Talmid

The Book of Job and the Song of Solomon

Translated Into English Metre

Talmid

The Book of Job and the Song of Solomon
Translated Into English Metre

ISBN/EAN: 9783337020583

Printed in Europe, USA, Canada, Australia, Japan

Cover: Foto ©Andreas Hilbeck / pixelio.de

More available books at **www.hansebooks.com**

THE BOOK OF JOB

AND

THE SONG OF SOLOMON.

THE BOOK OF JOB

AND

THE SONG OF SOLOMON

TRANSLATED INTO ENGLISH METRE

BY

T A L M I D

EDINBURGH

JAMES THIN, Publisher to the University

1890.

PREFACE.

UNDER a conviction that something might be done to
convey more accurately the structure and emphasis
of the Book of Job, the following attempt has been
made, and a metrical arrangement has been adopted
as in the Original Hebrew. No critical theories about
this booklet have been entered into; the one desire has
been to present a faithful translation. Decisive evidence
of value exists in its being found among the collected
Scriptures of the Old Testament; which were com-
municated to the Jews at various times, and were
preserved by that people until the coming of our Lord
Jesus Christ. He Himself used them, and gave to their
embodiment His unqualified approval, as a volume of
Divine authority, wisdom and revelation. Moreover
the man Job is twice mentioned in the 14th chapter of
Ezekiel as one of three most eminent persons; and in
the New Testament the Epistle of St James refers to the
patience of Job as a well known fact. The booklet of
Job therefore supplies an answer to the unsettling remark
that the Holy Scriptures, while they contain the Word of
God, are not throughout entitled to be so called. We,
the sinful children of Adam, do thus strive to undermine
the very firmest foundation; we hate the light and fight
against it, because our thoughts are evil. Nevertheless
the foundation standeth sure, "God who at sundry
times and in diverse manners spoke in time past unto
the fathers by the prophets, hath in these latter days

spoken unto us by His Son." "All Scripture was given by inspiration of God," and the selection of what is contained therein, whether history, law, or prophecy, all "is profitable for doctrine, for reproof, for correction, for instruction in righteousness, that the man of God may be perfect, thoroughly furnished unto all good works." We dare not doubt that the Divine Ruler knew how best to deal with His rebellious creatures, and it must be sad presumption for us to treat His Book with flippant objections or reckless speculations. If any one misunderstand or contradict the deeper secrets of Providence and Grace, let him consider how melancholy is the exhibition set forth in this booklet of Job; what ignorance, rashness, unfairness, bitterness, and self-conceit are in the hearts of even God-fearing men! Let him beware lest his misconduct should bring upon him the stern rebuke which Jehovah administered to Job and his friends in chapters xxxviii. 2, and xl. 2; and let him learn what St James Epistle v. 11 points out as a result of this narrative, that the end of the Lord is to be pitiful and merciful toward them who will humbly accept His chastisings and His instructions.

The warrant of inspiration must equally extend to the Song of Solomon. Frequently has this booklet been objected to by those who could not appreciate it, while on the contrary its spiritual applications have been greatly relished by innumerable excellent individuals. The Spirit of wisdom and holiness hath provided various kinds of food to suit various states of appetite, warning us from the vileness and danger of sin, and attracting us to the beauty and bliss of uprightness.

July 1890.

THE BOOK OF JOB.

THE BOOK OF JOB.

CHAPTER I.

(1.) THERE was a man in the land of Uz, whose name was Job; and that man was perfect and upright, and one who feared Great God, and turned from evil. (2.) And there were born to him seven sons and three daughters. (3.) And his possessions were seven thousand sheep, and three thousand camels, and five hundred yoke of oxen, and five hundred asses, and a very great household, so that this man was the greatest of all the sons of the East. (4.) And his sons went and made feast in house of each on his day; and they sent and called for their three sisters to eat and to drink with them. (5.) And it was so that when the days of feasting had gone round, Job would send and sanctify them; and he rose early in the morning, and did offer burnt offerings according to the number of them all; for Job said, " It may be that my sons did sin, and disown Great God in their hearts." Thus was Job doing all these days. (6.) Now there was a day when the sons of Great God came to present themselves before Jehovah, and Satan also came among them. (7.) And Jehovah said unto Satan, " From whence comest thou ?" and Satan answered to Jehovah and said, " From going up and down in the earth, and from walking about in it." (8.) And Jehovah said unto Satan, " Hast thou set thy heart toward My servant Job, that there is none like him in the earth, a man perfect and upright, fearing

A

I from my mother's belly, and naked must I return thither: Jehovah gave, and Jehovah hath taken away; may the name of Jehovah be blessed." (22.) In all this Job sinned not, nor was ascribing heedlessness to the Great God.

CHAPTER II.

(1.) AND there was a day when the sons of Great God came to present themselves before Jehovah, and Satan also came among them to present himself before Jehovah. (2.) And Jehovah said unto Satan, "From whence comest thou?" And Satan answered to Jehovah and said, "From going up and down in the earth, and from walking about in it." (3.) And Jehovah said unto Satan, "Hast thou set thy heart toward My servant Job, that there is none like him in the earth, a man perfect and upright, fearing Great God, and turning from evil; and still he is holding firm his integrity though thou wouldst move Me against him to swallow him up without cause?" (4.) And Satan answered to Jehovah and said, "A skin for a skin, and all which a man hath he will give for his soul. (5.) But do Thou put forth Thy hand, and touch his bone and his flesh, surely to Thy face he would disown Thee." (6.) And Jehovah said unto Satan, "Lo! he is in thy hand, but ah! to soul of him do thou give heed." (7.) So Satan went from presence of Jehovah, and smote Job with sore boils from the sole of his foot to the scalp of his head. (8.) And he took to him a potsherd to scrape himself therewith, and he was sitting among the ashes. (9.) Then said his wife to him, "Art thou still holding firm thine integrity? Disown Great God, and die." (10.) But he said unto her, "Thou speakest as one of the foolish women speaketh. What! shall we receive good from the Great God, and shall we not receive evil?" In all this

Job sinned not with his lips. (11.) Now when Job's three friends heard of all this evil which had come upon him, they came each from his own place, Eliphaz the Temanite, and Bildad the Shuhite, and Zophar the Naamathite; for they had appointed together to come to pity him, and to comfort him. (12.) And they lifted up their eyes from afar, but could not recognise him; and they lifted up their voices and wept; and they rent each one his mantle, and sprinkled dust over their heads toward heaven. (13.) And they sat with him on the earth seven days and seven nights, and no one spake a word to him, for they saw that the pain was exceeding great.

CHAPTER III.

1. AFTER this Job opened his mouth, and reviled his day:
2. And Job answered and said;
3. Let the day perish wherein I was born,
   And night which said, a man hath been conceived.
4. As for that very day, may it be dark;
   May God from his high place require it not;
   And may no gleam be shining forth on it;
5. Let darkness and deathshade lay claim to it;
   Let there be dwelling upon it a cloud;
   Let blacknesses of day be frighting it.
6. As for that night, may gloominess take it;
   Let it not be conjoined with days of year;
   Into the count of months may it not come.
7. Behold! let that same night be dreariness;
   Let there come into it no cheerful sound.
8. Let those speak ill of it who curse the day,
   Who are prepared to rouse up Leviathan.
9. Dark may the starring of its twilight be;
   Let it await for light which never comes,

Nor may it see the eyelids of a dawn.
10. For it closed not on me the belly's doors,
    Nor would hide misery from eyes of me.
11. Wherefore might I not from the womb have died?
    From belly have come forth, but to expire?
12. Why had there been the knees in front of me?
    And why were there the breasts that I should suck?
13. For now had I been laid, and would be still;
    I had been sleeping; then would I have rest,
14. Along with kings and counsellors of earth,
    · Those who do build dry places for themselves;
15. Or else along with princes who had gold,
    Who had with silver made their houses full;
16. Or like abortion hid, I would be dead;
    Like infants who had never seen the light.
17. There have the wicked from their troubling ceased,
    And there will rest the weariers of strength:
18. Together prisoners remain secure;
    They have not heard the voice of taskmaster:
19. The small as well as great, each one is there;
    And servant is a freedman from his lords.
20. Why should He give to wretched toiler light?
    And life to those who be of bitter soul?
21. Who long for death, while yet it cometh not,
    And who would dig it more than hidden stores;
22. Who gladdening almost to joyfulness
    Would be rejoiced when they could find a grave:
23. Or to a man the way of whom is hid,
    And about whom God will keep up a shade?
24. Yea, even while I feed, my sighing comes;
    And forth like water will my roarings pour.
25. For dread I dreaded doth arrive to me,
    And what I was afraid of comes to me.
26. I was not easy, neither was I still;
    Neither was I at rest, yet troubling comes.

CHAPTER IV.

1. THEN answered Eliphaz the Temanite and said :
2. Hath aught been testing thee, that thou art faint ?
   Yet who can bear restraint in argument ?
3. Behold ! thou hast instructed many men,
   And hands of slackness thou wouldst render firm.
4. Thy speech would cause the stumbling one to rise,
   And thou wouldst strengthen the down-bowing knees.
5. But now it comes to thee, and thou art faint ;
   It reaches thee, and thou art troubled sore.
6. Hast thou not reverence and confidence,
   Thine expectation, and thy perfect ways ?
7. O think ! what man in innocence was lost ?
   Or where have upright men been hid away ?
8. As I have seen, men plowing godlessness,
   And sowing misery, shall reap the same.
9. From breath of God they shall be perishing ;
   And from His wind of anger they shall fail.
10. The lion's roaring, and the jackal's voice,
    And teeth of younger lions are deranged :
11. Old lion perishing for want of prey :
    And whelps of lioness will scatter wide.
12. And toward me a something would steal up,
    Also mine ear would catch a hint of it.
13. In swaying thoughts from visions of the night,
    When falls a deep sleep upon feeble men ;
14. A dread came on me, and a tremblingness,
    And it disturbed my bones most dreadfully ;
15. Also a wind upon my face would pass ;
    Would bristle up the hair upon my flesh.
16. There stood, but its appearance I knew not,
    A strange similitude before mine eyes.
    Stillness there was and I could hear a voice

17. "Shall feeble man be righteous beyond God?
    Beyond his Maker can a man be clean?

18. Lo! in His servants He will not believe,
    And on His angels chargeth foolishness.

19. Yea, those who dwell in houses of mere clay,
    Such as have their foundations in the dust,
    They shall be crushing them before the moth;

20. From morn to eve they shall be beaten down;
    Without resort they perish utterly.

21. Is not their surplus gone away with them?
    They shall die off, and with no wise result."

CHAPTER V.

1. CALL now! will there be one to answer thee?
   And toward whom of holies wilt thou turn?

2. For to a fool provokingness may slay;
   And envy may drive simpleton to death.

3. I, I have seen a foolish man take root,
   And I would mark his homestead suddenly.

4. Far off from safety would his children be;
   And would be crusht in gate, none rescuing.

5. His very harvest shall a starveling eat,
   Yea, to the thorns will he be taking it;
   And a designer panteth for his wealth.

6. Though from the dust shall not come godlessness,
   Nor from the ground will misery spring up,

7. Yet mankind will to misery be born;
   And burning sparks will make high upward flight.

8. But I, I shall be seeking toward God,
   And to Great God I will commit my case;

9. The doer of great things beyond a search,
   Of wondrous things which are beyond recount:

10. He who gives rain upon the face of earth,
    And sendeth waters on the face of fields,

11. To put the lowly ones on lofty place,
     And mourning ones are safely set on high :
12. He foils the projectings of crafty men,
     So that their hands do nought efficiently ;
13. He catcheth wise men in their craftiness,
     And counsels of the crooked are made rash ;
14. By day they will be meeting darknesses,
     And like the night they grope at brilliant noon :
15. But He will save from sword out of their mouth,
     Also from grasping hand, the needy man.
16. So may the meek one have expectancy,
     And so injustice hath closed up its mouth.
17.   Behold ! how happy he,
     The mortal man whom God doth hold in check ;
     Almighty's discipline reject not thou.
18. For He, He maketh sore, and bindeth up ;
     He strikes a wound, and His hands will make whole.
19. In six distresses He will rescue thee ;
     Also in seven shall no ill touch thee :
20. In famine He redeemeth thee from death,
     Also in war from the attacking sword :
21. From scourging of a tongue shalt thou be hid,
     And shalt not fear despoiling though it come.
22. At spoiling and at humbling thou wilt laugh ;
     From animals of earth mayst thou fear nought ;
23. For with the stones of field thou hast a league,
     And animals of field keep peace with thee.
24. And thou dost know that peace is in thy tent ;
     Thou visitest thy home, and wilt not sin ;
25. And knowest that thy seed shall multiply,
     Thine offspring be like herbage of the earth.
26. Thou shalt go in with fitness to the grave,
     Like laying up of corn-heap in its time.
27. Lo ! this we have searched out ; it must be so :
     Hear it, and know it fully for thyself.

CHAPTER VI.

1. THEN answered Job and said :
2. O that were weighed with strictness my provoke,
   And my downthrow were laid in scales at once !
3. For now it is more heavy than sea sand ;
   Therefore my words are fully warranted.
4. For arrows of Almighty round me come,
   Whereof the poison doth my spirit drink ;
   The frights of God array themselves at me.
5. Will the wild ass bray over tender herb ?
   Or will the ox low o'er his provender ?
6. What thing insipid eat we without salt ?
   Or is there sense in drivelling of dreams ?
7. Things which my appetite refused to touch,
   These like my languishing are now my food.
8. Who will give speedy grant of my request ?
   And my expectance, oh that God would give !
9. Even may God be pleased to crush me down !
   May He let loose His hand and cut me off !
10. And there would still be comforting for me,
    And I would bear in pain ; He might not spare ;
    For I had hid no words of Holy One.
11. What is my strength that I should have a hope ?
    And what mine end that I should stretch my soul ?
12. Although a strength of stones had been my strength,
    Or had my flesh been brass,
13. Yet surely there is not my help in me.
    Also efficiency is driven from me.
14. To humbled man his friend owes kindliness,
    Or the Almighty's fear he might forsake.
15. My brethren have been traitors like a brook ;
    Like the strong gush of brooks they will pass off ;
16. Those which are black by reason of the ice,

Along by which the snow will hide itself:

17. In time of parching they will be reduced;
    When hot, they are extinguished from their place.

18. The caravans will turn aside their way;
    They will go up through wastes, and will be lost.

19. The caravans of Tema have looked out;
    The Sheba travellers did wait for them;

20. They are ashamed because of confidence;
    They have come on thus far, and are dismayed.

21. So at this time have ye been to myself;
    Ye see a casting down, and ye will fear.

22. Is it because I said, "Give ye to me"?
    Or, "From your strength pay ye a bribe for me,"

23. Or, "O do ye free me from troubler's hand,"
    Or, "From tyrannic hands redeem ye me"?

24. O point ye me and I will hold my peace;
    And how I erred, cause me to understand.

25. How forcible are sayings of right sort!
    But what doth argument of yours reprove?

26. Are for reproof the speeches you devise?
    But for mere wind the sayings of despair?

27. Yea, on an orphan ye would cause a fall,
    And would be bargaining against your friend.

28. But now be ye content; turn ye to me,
    And to the face of you I shall not lie.

29. Pray do return! let no injustice be;
    And still return, my righteousness is here.

30. Is there in my tongue anything unjust?
    Cannot my palate be discerning wrongs?

CHAPTER VII.

1. Is it not wartime for frail man on earth?
   And like the days of hireling are his days.

2. As servant will pant earnestly for shade,

And as a hireling will await his work;

3. So I must take my months of worthlessness,
   And nights of misery keep count for me.

4. If I were lying down, then have I said,
   " When shall I rise ? " but measured long was eve,
   And filled was I with tossings till the dawn.

5. Clothed is my flesh with worms and clods of dust ;
   My skin breaks short, and loathsome it will be.

6. My days go swifter than a weaver's loom,
   And they will fail as expectation ends.

7. Remember Thou that spirit is my life ;
   Mine eye will not return to seeing good.

8. No eye which saw me will keep view of me ;
   Thine eyes are on me when I shall not be.

9. Failing hath been a cloud, and off it moves ;
   But goer down to Sheol comes not up.

10. He shall no more return to his own house,
    And no more shall his place acknowledge him.

11. But I, yea, I will not refrain my mouth ;
    I shall in trouble of my spirit speak ;
    I shall complain in bitterness of soul.

12. Am I a sea, or any monstrous brute,
    That Thou wilt settle over me a watch ?

13. When I did say, " My couch will comfort me,
    My bed will give relief in my complaint ; "

14. Then Thou hast been down-casting me with dreams,
    Also by visions Thou wilt frighten me.

15. Of strangulation would my soul make choice,
    Preferring death to my embodiment.

16. I do reject.   Not always would I live.
    Cease Thou from me ; my days are vanity.

17. What is frail man that Thou shouldst make him great,
    And that Thou settest toward him Thy heart ?

18. And wilt revisit him at morning-tides,
    At every moment wilt be trying him ?

19. How long wilt Thou not look away from me?
    Wilt Thou not let me swallow down my spit?
20. Oh! I have sinned : what may I do for Thee,
        Close watcher of mankind?
    Why hast Thou set me as a butt for Thee,
    And I become a burden on myself?
21. And why forgiv'st Thou not my trespassing,
    Removing mine iniquity away?
    For now I to the dust would be laid down ;
    And Thou mightst seek me, but I should not be.

CHAPTER VIII.

1. THEN answered Bildad the Shuhite, and said :
2. How long wilt thou be speaking of these things,
   And blustering wind be sayings of thy mouth?
3. Will God be doing judgement perversely?
   And the Almighty be perverting right?
4. Although thy children did sin against Him,
   And He sent them to their transgression's grasp ;
5. If thou thyself wouldst early seek to God,
   And to the Almighty thou wouldst supplicate ;
6. If pure and upright thou be really,
   Then surely now He would arouse for thee,
   And prosper homestead of thy righteousness.
7. Though thy beginning had been only small,
   Thy latter end would grow exceedingly.
8. For ask, I pray thee, of the former race,
   And set thyself to search their forefathers ;
9. Since yesterday came we, and nought we know ;
   Since but a shadow are our days on earth ;
10. Would these not point thee? they would say to thee,
    And from their hearts would they make speech go
        forth.
11. Will bulrush grow up stately without mire?

Will reed of meadow spread when waters fail?

12. While yet in freshness it may be unpluckt,
    But it before all grass will wither down.
13. So are the paths of all forgetting God;
    And hypocrite's expectance shall be lost.
14. Whoever will abuse his hardihood,
    While house of spider is his place of trust;
15. He on his house may lean, but shall not stand,
    May firmly grasp it, but he shall not rise.
16. Though wetted he may be before the sun,
    And o'er his garden may his suckers go,
17. Around a fountain may his roots be wrapt,
    A house of stones he may be gazing at;
18. Yet He will swallow him out of his place,
    And it denies him, "I have not seen thee."
19. Lo! such is the enjoyment of his way;
    But from the dust will other ones spring up.
20. Lo! God will not reject a perfect man;
    Nor will He grasp the hand of evil men.
21. Still He will fill with laughter thine own mouth,
    Also thy lips with a rejoicing shout.
22. Those hating Thee shall clothe themselves with shame
    And tent of wicked men shall cease to be.

CHAPTER IX.

1. THEN answered Job, and said:
2. Assuredly I know that thus it is;
   But how can feeble man be just with God?
3. If he delight to be at strife with Him,
   He answers Him not one of thousand things.
4. The wise in heart, and masterful of strength!
   Who hath grown hard to Him, and will have peace?
5. He who removeth mountains unawares,
   When He o'erturns them in His angriness;

6. He who doth shake the earth out of its place,
   And pillars thereof show their tremblingness ;
7. Who sayeth, and the sun will not arise ;
   And who about the stars will put a seal ;
8. He who alone doth stretch the heavens out,
   And treadeth on the lofty waves of sea ;
9. Who makes the Bear, Orion, Pleiades,
          And inner chambers of the south ;
10. Who doeth acts most great and beyond search,
    Things wonderful which are beyond recount.
11. Lo ! He may cross near me, though I see not ;
    And may pass on, though I perceive Him not.
12. Lo ! when He snatcheth, who will turn Him back ?
    Or who will say to Him, "What doest Thou ?"
13. Ah ! God will not withdraw His angriness ;
    Beneath Him bowed the helpers of Rahab.
14. Much less could I myself be answering Him,
    Could I be choosing out my words with Him.
15. Since were I righteous, I would not reply ;
    To Him who judgeth I must supplicate.
16. Though I had called, and He would answer me,
    I scarce believe that He would hear my voice,
17. While with a tempest He is bruising me,
    And multiplies my wounds without a cause.
18. He will not let me bring my spirit back,
    But He will surfeit me with bitter things.
19. Yea, as to strength, the Masterful behold !
    And as to judgement, who would fix my time ?
20. Though righteous, yet my mouth would prove my
          wrong ;
    Perfect am I ? it would prove me perverse.
21. Perfect were I, I would not know my soul ;
          I would reject my life.
22. One and the same is He ; therefore I said,
    " Perfect and wicked men doth He consume."

23. Suppose a scourge might cause death suddenly,
    At testing of the innocent it mocks.
24. The earth is placed in hand of wicked man ;
    Its judges' faces He will cover up ;
    If not His angriness, whose may it be ?
25. Also my days go swifter than a post ;
    They have fled off, they saw no coming good.
26. They did pass off along with ships of speed,
    As vulture will swoop down upon its food.
27. If I said, now forgetting my complaint,
    I shall forsake my looks, and brighten up ;
28. I was afraid of all my grievous deeds ;
    I knew Thou wilt not hold me innocent.
29.   Myself, I would be wicked ;
    Why thus should I be vainly labouring ?
30. Though I might wash myself in melted snow,
    And I had purified with soap my hands ;
31. Then in the ditch mightst Thou be plunging me,
    And mine own clothes would be abhorring me.
32. Since no man such as I may answer Him :
    Let us together into judgement come.
33. There is not any umpire between us ;
    One who might lay his hand upon us both.
34. Let Him remove from upon me His rod ;
    And may His terror not be frighting me.
35. I fain would speak, and not be fearing Him ;
    But such is not the present case with me.

CHAPTER X.

1. DISHEARTENED hath my soul been by my life
   I fain would leave complaint upon myself,
   I shall speak out in bitterness of soul.
2. I will say unto God, "Condemn me not

Cause me to know why Thou wilt strive with me.

3. Can it be good to Thee that Thou oppress?
   That Thou reject the labour of Thy hands?
   And that on wicked counsels Thou wilt shine?

4. 　　　Hast Thou got eyes of flesh?
   Or wilt Thou see as feeble man doth see?

5. Are Thy days like the days of feeble man?
   Are Thy years like the days of stronger man?

6. That Thou wilt seek for mine iniquity,
   And for my sinfulness Thou wilt enquire?

7. Though thou dost know that wicked I am not,
   And from Thy hand there is no rescuer.

8. Thy hands took pains with me, and wrought me out,
   Knit round about, yet Thou wilt swallow me.

9. O think, that like the clay Thou wroughtest me,
   And toward dust Thou mayest send me back.

10. Didst Thou not cause me to be poured like milk,
    And also cause me to congeal like cheese?

11. With skin and flesh Thou wouldst cause me to clothe,
    And bones and sinews Thou didst fence me with.

12. Thou wroughtest with me life and kindliness,
    And o'er my spirit did Thy visits watch;

13. And these things Thou didst store within Thy heart,
    And I have known that this hath been with Thee.

14. If I did sin, then Thou didst notice me,
    And from iniquity wouldst not clear me.

15. If I were wicked, ah! then woe to me!
    Or righteous, I would not lift up my head;
    Outdone with buffets, see Thou my distress!

16. And it will grow!　Like jackal Thou hunt'st me;
    And wilt again act wondrously on me;

17. Thou wilt renew Thy witness before me,
    And art increasingly provoked with me;
    Changes and warfare keep me company.

18. So why from womb didst Thou make me come forth

I might expire, and no eye would see me.

19. As though I had not been, I might be now;
     From belly to the grave had I been led.

20. Are not my days but few? so do Thou cease,
     And part from me, that I may cheer somewhat,

21. Before I must go hence, without return,
     Toward the land of darkness and death-shade;

22. A land as dark as utter gloominess;
     A death-shade where there are no guiding signs,
     And shining is as utter gloominess."

CHAPTER XI.

1. THEN answered Zophar the Naamathite, and said:

2. Shall multitude of words get no reply?
   And shall a man of talk be justified?

3. Shall thy assertions make men hold their peace,
   And thou wilt mock, while none assigns disgrace?

4. And thou art saying, "Pure my doctrine is,
   And clean have I been in the eyes of Thee."

5. But oh! that we could get a word from God,
   And He would open His own lips with thee!

6. And show unto thee wisdom's secret things,
   That these are doublings of effectiveness!
   So do thou know that God
   Exacteth less than thine iniquity.

7. A searching-out of God, how canst thou find?
   Or the Almighty, canst thou fully find?

8. The heights of heavens, ah! what canst thou do?
   More deep than Sheol, ah! what canst thou know?

9. It longer is than earth in measurement,
   Also it must be broader than the sea.

10. If He should cause a change, a shutting-up,
    Or an assembly, who may turn Him back?

11. For He, He knoweth mortal worthlessness,

B

And may see falseness, but may not regard.
12. Yet hollow man may be made full of heart;
    Though wild ass colt will human-kind be born.
13. If thou thyself hast firmly set thy heart,
    And hast been spreading toward Him thy palms;
14. If wrong be in thy hand, put it far off;
    Nor let injustice dwell within thy tents.
15. For then mayst thou lift up a spotless face;
    And being stedfast, thou mayst have no fear.
16. Then thou, of misery thou mayst forget;
    As waters past shall thy remembrance be:
17. And more than brilliant noon shall lifetime rise;
    Thou shalt fly forth; like morning shalt thou be:
18. And thou shalt trust in true expectancy,
    And having dug, shalt trustfully lie down;
19. And couch thy flock where none shall cause alarm:
    And many have been those who court thy smile.
20. Whereas the eyes of wicked men shall fail;
    And place of refuge hath been lost from them;
    And their expectance is to breathe out soul.

CHAPTER XII.

1. Then answered Job, and said;
2. Assuredly yourselves must be the folk,
   Also along with you must wisdom die.
3. Moreover, I have heart as well as you;
   No whit inferior am I to you.
   Also with whom are not such things as these?
4. A laughing-stock to neighbours I may be;
   Who calls to God, and He will answer him;
   A laughing-stock is righteous perfect man.
5. A torch despised in thoughts of self secure
   Is one who oft hath slippings of the foot.
6. At ease will be the tents of plunderers,

And careless will be those who trouble God
As to what God did bring to hand of each.

7. But do thou ask the beast, it will point thee ;
   And bird of heaven, it will show to thee ;

8. Or muse thou of the earth, it will point thee ;
   And tell to thee will fishes of the deep.

9. Who doth not know by all such things as these,
   It was Jehovah's hand which wrought out this ?

10. Since in the hand of Him is each live soul,
    Also the spirit of all flesh of man.

11. Will not the ear be trier of discourse ?
    Also the palate taster of its food ?

12. In very aged men is wisdom found ;
    And length of days produceth skilfulness.

13. With Him are wisdom, also mightiness ;
    To Him are counsel, also skilfulness.

14. Lo ! He may wreck, and it shall not be built ;
    May shut against a man, and none may ope.

15. Lo ! He stints waters, and they will dry up ;
    Or sends them forth, and they upturn the earth.

16. With Him are power, and efficiency ;
    To Him belong misleader and misled.

17. He causeth counsellors to go despoiled,
    Also the judges He makes crazy fools.

18. The discipline of kings He hath thrown loose,
    And He will bind a girdle on their loins.

19. He causeth priests to go away despoiled,
    And men of firmness He will overthrow.

20. He doth remove the lip of faithful men ;
    And sense of elders He will take away.

21. He poureth a contempt on potentates,
    And belt of gushing youths he hath made slack.

22. He doth reveal deep things out of the dark,
    And will bring out to lightness the deathshade.

23. He maketh nations spread, or makes them nought ;

He straggles nations round, or leads them on ;
24. Removes the heart of heads of folk of earth ;
 And makes them wander without aim or way.
25. They shall grope darkly, without any light ;
 He will cause them to wander like drunk men.

CHAPTER XIII.

1. Lo ! the whole matter hath mine own eye seen ;
 Mine ear did hear, and was discerning it.
2. As ye have known, I do know, even I ;
 No whit inferior am I to you.
3. But I, to the Almighty I would speak,
 And would delight in reasoning with God.
4. Whereas yourselves are forging falsity ;
 Physicians of no value are ye all.
5. O that ye would entirely hold your peace !
 And it would be for wisdom unto you.
6. O do ye listen to my reasoning !
 To pleadings of my lips do ye give heed !
7. Is it for God ye speak what is unjust ?
 Also for Him that ye speak guilefully ?
8. Is it His personage that ye respect ?
 Is it for mighty God that ye will strive ?
9. Would it be good that He should search out you ?
 Would ye, like gameful men, make game with Him ?
10. Most sharply He would be reproving you,
 If ye in secret favour personage.
11. Would not His dignity be frighting you ?
 And dread of Him be falling down on you ?
12. Your memories are proverbs of mere ash ;
 For mounds of merest clay will be your mounds.
13. Keep ye your peace from me, and I will speak,
 Yea I, and let there come on me what may.
14. For what lift I my flesh into my teeth ?

Also my soul put I, into my hand?

15. Lo! He may kill me; I may have no hope:
But ah! my ways I would to Him discuss.

16. Moreover He may be my saving help,
Though to His face no hypocrite may come,

17. Do ye be hearing carefully my speech,
Also my declaration, with your ears.

18. Behold, pray! how I have arrayed the cause;
I know that I, I shall be justified.

19. Who may be he that will contend with me?
For now I would keep silence, and expire.

20. Ah! two things do not Thou perform with me;
Then from Thy presence I would not be hid.

21. Thine hand from off me do Thou take afar;
And may Thy terror not be frighting me.

22. But call Thou; and I, I will give reply;
Or let me speak, and do Thou charge me back.

23. How great were mine iniquities and sins?
My trespass and my sin make Thou me know.

24. Wherefore wilt Thou be keeping hid Thy face?
And think I am an enemy to Thee?

25. At driven leafage wilt Thou tyrannise?
And withered stubble wilt Thou persecute?

26. For Thou wilt write against me bitter things,
And make me heir my youth's iniquities;

27. And Thou wilt put into the stocks my feet;
And Thou wilt be observing all my paths;
On my feet roots Thou wilt inscribe Thy mark.

28. And he, like rotten thing, shall wear away;
Like garment which is eaten by the moth.

CHAPTER XIV.

1. MAN who is born of woman
Is short of days, and full of restlessness.

2. Like bloom he did come forth, and shall be mown ;
   He fleeth like a shade, and shall not stand.
3. Yea, upon such hast Thou kept open eyes
   And wilt bring me in judgement with Thyself.
4. Who will give clean thing out of an unclean ?
   Not any one.
5. Surely determined are the days of him ;
   The number of his new moons is with Thee ;
   His limit made by Thee he cannot pass.
6. Look Thou away from him, and let him cease,
   Till like a hireling he may please his day.
7. For of a tree there is expectancy,
   Though it should be cut down, it still may change,
   Also the suckers thereof may not cease.
8. Though aged in the earth may be its root,
   And in the dust the stump thereof may die,
9. It through the scent of water may sprout up,
   And hath made harvest-cropping like a plant.
10. But strong man is to die, and become weak ;
    And each man will expire, and where is he ?
11. Off from the sea have waters gone their way,
    And river will be shrunk, and hath dried up.
12. And man lies down, and he shall not arise ;
    Till heavens be no more they shall not wake ;
    Nor shall they be aroused out of their sleep.
13. Oh that in Sheol Thou wouldst have me stored !
    Wouldst hide me till Thine anger be withdrawn,
    Wouldst set my limit, and remember me !
14. Though a strong man must die, may he have life ?
    All days of this my warfare I will hope
    Until arrival of my coming change.
15. Thou wilt call, and I, I will answer Thee ;
    To Thy hands-work Thou shouldst have strong
        desire,
16. But now my steps Thou wilt be numbering ;

Wilt Thou not be observing on my sin?

17. Sealed in a bag hath been my trespassing;
    And Thou wilt fix o'er mine iniquity.

18. Yet mountain when it falls will crumble down;
    And rock may be removing from its place;

19. The stones are by the waters beaten down;
    The dust of earth sweeps off its coming crops;
    And man's expectancy Thou hast destroyed.

20. Thou wilt o'erpower him fully, and he goes;
    Wilt change his look, and wilt send him away.

21. His sons get honour, but he will not know;
    Or may lack growth, but he feels not for them.

22. Ah! his own flesh upon him will give pain;
    Also his soul upon himself shall mourn.

CHAPTER XV.

1. THEN answered Eliphaz the Temanite, and said;

2. Should wise man answer knowledge that is puffed?
   And should he fill his belly with east wind?

3. Discussing matter which can profit naught,
   And speeches with no usefulness in them.

4. Yea, thou thyself wouldst cast off reverence,
   And wilt restrain communion before God.

5. For thine iniquity will sway thy mouth;
   And thou wilt choose the tongue of crafty men.

6. Thine own mouth will condemn thee, and not I;
   And thine own lips will answer against thee.

7. Art thou the first of mankind who was born?
   Before the little hills wast thou brought forth?

8. In secret of God's council wouldst thou hear,
   And be restraining wisdom to thyself?

9. What hast thou known, which we know nothing of?
   Perceivest thou that which is not with us?

10. With us are both greyhead, and aged man,

More than thy father plentiful in days.

11. Are comfortings from God too small for thee?
And may a something gentle be with thee?

12. To what will thine own heart be taking thee?
And what height will thine eyes be aiming at?

13. That thou wouldst send thy spirit back to God,
And hast put forth such speaking from thy mouth.

14. What is frail man that he should become pure?
And that one born of woman should be just?

15. Behold! He in His saints will not believe;
Nor have the heavens pureness in his sight:

16. Much more abominably vile is man
Who drinks injustice like a water draft!

17. I will inform thee; listen thou to me;
What I have gazed at, I would fain recount;

18. Those things which wise men would be showing
forth,
And kept not hidden, from their forefathers;

19. To whom, to whom alone the land was given;
And there had passed no stranger through their
midst.

20. All days of wicked man he pains himself,
And for a tyrant few years have been stored.

21. A sound of dreaded men is in his ears;
Mid peace a spoiler shall come in on him.

22. He has no faith in getting back from dark;
But closely watched hath he been for the sword.

23. Flitting about is he for bread: "Where next?"
He knows that his own hand brought darksome day.

24. Affright him will distress and anguishment:
Thou wilt o'erpower him as a warlike king.

25. For he did stretch out toward God his hand;
And to the Almighty he would brag himself:

26. He would be running toward Him with neck,
With thickness of the bosses of his shields.

27. For covered is his face with his own fat,
     And he would make strong lining on his flank.
28. But he shall dwell in cities hid away,
     In houses having no inhabitants,
     Such as were speedily becoming heaps.
29. Not rich is he, nor shall his force arise;
     Nor shall extend to earth their influence.
30. Out from the darkness he shall not depart;
     His suckers shall persistent flame dry up;
     And he departs with spirit of His mouth.
31. Let no strayed man believe in worthlessness,
     For worthless truly would be his exchange.
32. Ere his day endeth, it shall be fulfilled,
     And frond of him shall not be flourishing.
33. He is like vine with fruit exceeding sour;
     And like an olive which casts off its bloom.
34. For dreary shall be hypocrite's resort,
     And fire hath eaten tents of bribery.
35. Conceiving mischief, breeding godlessness,
     Also their belly will confirm deceit.

CHAPTER XVI.

1. THEN answered Job, and said;
2. I have been hearing many things like these:
     O wretched comforters are all of you!
3. Is there an end to words of puffiness?
     Or what emboldens thee to answer so?
4. Yea, I myself, like you, am fain to speak;
     If your soul were instead of mine own soul,
     I would be joining beside you in speech,
     And I would shake beside you with my head.
5. I would be strengthening you with my mouth;
     And movement of my lips would offer ease.
6. If I do speak, not eased will be my pain;

And if I do cease, what from me would go?

7. Ah, now! He hath been causing me to faint :
Thou hast made desolate all my resort ;

8. And wouldst arrest me ; witness it hath been ;
Also my failure rising up in me
      Will answer in my face.

9. His anger tore, and He opposeth me ;
He hath been gnashing against me His teeth ;
My troubler, he will whet his eyes at me.

10. They have been gaping at me with their mouth ;
They in reproach have smitten me on cheeks ;
Together against me they fill themselves.

11. God would consign me to a foolish man,
And turn me upon hands of wicked men.

12. At ease was I, but He would lash me loose ;
Hold me by neck, and would shake me to shreds ;
He makes me stand as target for Himself.

13. All round against me would His archers come ;
He would split through my reins, and would not
      spare ;
He would be pouring to the earth my gall ;

14. He would be breaching me with breach on breach ;
Would run upon me like a mighty man.

15. Sackcloth have I been sewing o'er my skin,
And have been rolling in the dust my horn.

16. My face with weeping hath become inflamed,
And o'er mine eyelids is the shade of death ;

17. For nothing violent in mine own hands ;
But mine own praying was with purity.

18. O earth ! be not thou covering my blood ;
Nor let there be a place for mine outcry.

19. Yea, now behold ! in heaven my witness is,
Also my voucher is in heights above.

20.   Though scornful be my friends,
Yet toward God mine eye hath dropping been ;

21. And one may reason for strong man with God,
    As may a son of Adam for his friend.
22 Since years but few in number shall arrive,
    And path with no returning I must go.

CHAPTER XVII.

1. My spirit hath been bound ; my days run out ;
    Graves are for me,
2. Surely there must be gameful men with me,
    In whose embitterings mine eye must lodge.
3. O do Thou fix ! engage me with Thyself ;
    Where may be he who will strike hands with me ?
4. Since Thou hast stared their heart from wise-doing,
    Therefore Thou wilt not be exalting them.
5. For flattery may one make show of friends,
    But eyes of his posterity shall fail.
6. And He sets me for byword of the folks,
    And openly dishonoured I must be ;
7. And dim from provocation is mine eye,
    So are my limbs like shadow, all of them.
8. Astonished will upright man be at this ;
    And innocent at hypocrite will rouse :
9. And righteous man will firmly hold his way ;
    And man who hath clean hands will add to strength
10. But all of these, return ye and do come,
    And I shall find no wise man among you.
11. My days have passed, my purposes are snapt,
    Possessions of my heart !
12. A night they will be putting to a day ;
    The light is near from presence of the dark.
13. I do expect that Sheol is my house ;
    I in the darkness have spread out my bed.
14. I to the ditch did call, " my father thou ! "
    " My mother and my sister ! " to the worms.

15. And where now should be my expectancy ?
    Yea, my expectance, who will have its view ?
16. To parts of Sheol they shall downward go
    When we together on the dust are laid.

CHAPTER XVIII.

1. THEN answered Bildad the Shuhite, and said ;
2. Till when will ye be setting blocks to speech ?
    May you discern, thereafter we will talk.
3. Wherefore should we be reckoned like the beast ?
    Should we unclean be in the eyes of you ?
4. Tearing his own soul in his angriness,
    Is earth to be forsaken to suit thee ?
    And rock to be removing from its place ?
5. Nay, light of wicked men shall go extinct ;
    Neither will shine the kindling of his fire.
6. The light hath darkened in the tent of him ;
    Also his lamp beside him goes extinct.
7. Straitened shall steppings of his vigour be ;
    And his own counselling shall cast him forth.
8. For, sent into a net by his own feet,
    He on entanglement shall walk about ;
9. A trap will firmly hold him by the heel ;
    And against him designer will prevail :
10. Down-hidden in the earth shall be his cord ;
    Also his capturings upon the road.
11. Around will terrors be affrighting him,
    And will cause him to hurry to his feet.
12. Enfamisht shall the vigour of him be ;
    Calamity is ready for his limp.
13. Devouring bit by bit the skin of him,
    Devour him bit by bit shall death's firstborn.
14. Pluckt from his tent shall be his confidence,
    And it will march him to the king of terrors.

15. It shall dwell in his tent without himself ;
    Outspread upon his home shall brimstone be.
16. Beneath shall roots of him be drying up,
    Also above, his branches shall be cropt.
17. His memory hath perisht from the earth,
    And no name is for him upon the street.
18. They shall drive him from light toward the dark,
    And from the world they will chase him away.
19. No son hath he, nor nephew with his folk ;
    No one remaining where he did sojourn.
20. At his day have those after been amazed ;
    And those before had taken hold of fright.
21. Ah ! such are dwellings of unrighteous man,
    And this the place is which hath not known God.

CHAPTER XIX.

1. THEN answered Job, and said ;
2. Till when will ye be wearying my soul ?
   And will ye be down-crushing me with words ?
3. These ten times ye would be disgracing me ;
   Ye feel no shame in acting strange to me.
4. But though assuredly I must have erred,
   'Tis with myself my error will remain.
5. If ye indeed against me will wax great,
   And will discuss against me my reproach,
6. Know ye at once that God subverteth me,
   And that his net hath been encircling me.
7. Lo ! I cry violence, but am not heard ;
   I cry for help, but judgement cometh not.
8. My path He fenced so that I cannot pass,
   And on my footways darkness He will set.
9. My glory from upon me He hath stript,
   And will remove the crowning of my head ;
10. Will break me down around, and I must go,

And my expectance flitteth like a tree.

11. So hot against me grew His angriness,
　　He thinks of me as of those troubling Him.

12. Together will His troops be coming in,
　　And will be raising against me their way,
　　And will be camping round about my tent.

13. My brothers from me He hath put afar;
　　Those knowing me, ah! are estranged from me;

14. 　　　My kinsfolk have left off,
　　And my acquaintances forgotten me.

15. 　　　Sojourners of my house,
　　And my handmaids for stranger reckon me;
　　An alien I have been in eyes of them.

16. I called my servant, but he answered not;
　　I with my mouth must be entreating him.

17. My spirit is grown strange to mine own wife,
　　Though I showed grace to our own progeny.

18. Yea, tender lads have been rejecting me;
　　I fain would rise, but they will speak at me.

19. Abhorring me are all my council men,
　　And those I loved are turning against me.

20. Unto my skin and flesh my bone doth cling,
　　And I would fain escape with skin of teeth.

21. Show grace to me, show grace, O ye my friends!
　　Because the hand of God is touching me,

22. Why will ye persecute me as doth God?
　　And from my flesh are ye not satisfied?

23. O that at once my words were written down!
　　O that they in a book might be inscribed!

24. Even with pen of iron and with lead
　　May they for ever on the rock be hewn!

25. And I, I know that my Redeemer lives,
　　And afterward he on the dust will rise.

26. And after enemies have cleared off this,
　　Yet I from mine own flesh will gaze on God,

27. Whom I, yea I will gaze on for myself,
    And mine own eyes have seen ; no stranger then.
    Failing have been my reins within my breast,
28. Because ye say, "How we will pester him !"
    Though root of matter hath been found in me.
29. Be shrinking for your own sakes from the sword,
    For wrathful are chastisings of the sword,
    That thereby ye may know what is redress.

CHAPTER XX.

1. THEN answered Zophar the Naamathite, and said :
2. Therefore my swaying thoughts will bring me back ;
   And for this reason is my haste in me.
3. Reproof of my disgracing I do hear ;
   And spirit from my skill will answer me.
4. Is this what thou hast known from olden time,
   From placing of mankind upon the earth ?
5. That cheerfulness of wicked men is short,
   And joy of hypocrite a moment lasts.
6. Though climb to heaven may his dignity,
   And though his head may to thick cloud reach up ;
7. He like his dung shall perish utterly ;
   Those who had seen him will say, " Where is he ? "
8. Like dream he flies, and they shall not find him ;
   He is slipt off like vision of the night.
9. An eye glared on him, but it cannot now ;
   And no more shall his place be viewing him.
10. His sons would diligently please poor folk
    And his own hands would bring his vigour back.
11. His members have been full of youthfulness ;
    But it with him upon the dust shall lie.
12. Though sweet within his mouth may evil be,
    And he may hide it underneath his tongue,
13. Though he may spare it, and forsake it not,

But will retain it in the palate's reach ;
14. His food in his own bowels hath been turned ;
    The gall of adders is inside of him.
15. Wealth he did swallow, but shall vomit it ;
    Out from his belly God will claim it back.
16. The venoming of adders he shall suck ;
    Or slaying him shall be the viper's tongue.
17. May he not see the runlets of the floods,
    The flowing brooks of honey and milk-curd !
18. Restoring labour, he shall swallow nought ;
    In worth of his exchange he shall not joy.
19. For he did crush, he did forsake poor folks ;
    A house he robbed, and would not build it up.
20. Since in his belly he had known no ease,
    He in his coveting let nought escape ;
21. There will be nothing left him to devour ;
    Therefore his good success shall not endure.
22. Mid his full striking, trouble is for him ;
    Each hand of wretchedness will come to him.
23. It shall be, when he fills his belly full,
    That He will send on him His anger's heat,
    And He will rain upon them while he feeds.
24. Off he will flee from armament of steel ;
    Through him shall penetrate a bow of brass :
25. He draws, and from the body it will come ;
    Yea, glistening out from his gall it goes ;
            Upon him terrors fall.
26. All darkly hidden-down shall be his stores ;
    A fire not blown shall be devouring him ;
    Ill doomed shall be the remnant in his tent.
27. The heavens will reveal his sinfulness ;
    Earth also will upraise herself at him.
28. Remove away will increase of his house,
    Forth pouring in His day of angriness.
29. Such portion wicked man hath from great God ;
    Such heritage Almighty doth decree.

CHAPTER XXI.

1. THEN answered Job, and said;
2. O will you hear attentively my speech,
   And O let this be for your comfortings!
3. Do bear with me, and I yea I will speak;
   And after I have spoken, thou mayst mock.
4. Do I, yea I to man make my complaint?
   And truly why may not my spirit fail?
5. Turn ye to me, and be astonished,
   And be ye laying hand upon your mouth.
6. When I did call to mind, I was sore vexed;
   And there did hold my flesh a shuddering dread.
7. Wherefore is it that wicked men will live,
   Have become old, yea mighty valiant ones?
8. Their seed established in their front with them,
   Also their offspring are before their eyes;
9. The houses of these men are quit of dread,
   Nor doth the rod of God come down on them.
10. Their bull hath gendered, and he will not fail;
    Their cow will calve, and will not be bereaved.
11. They will send forth like sheep their tender ones;
    And children of their own will skip and dance.
12. They will take up the timbrel and the harp,
    And will be gladdening at sound of pipe.
13. They will wear out in mirthfulness their days;
    And in a moment be to Sheol cast.
14. But they would say to God, " Depart from us;"
    "For knowledge of Thy ways delights not us:
15. "What is the Almighty that we should serve Him?
    "And of what use that we should meet with Him?"
16. Lo! not in their own hand is their success.
    Counsel of wicked men be far from me!
17. How oft goes lamp of wicked men extinct?

C

And will come on them their calamity ?
Cords He will portion in His angriness ;

18. Shall they be like to straw before a wind ?
And like to chaff which tempest steals away ?

19. God may store up his vigour for his sons ;
Let Him requite to him, and he shall know.

20. Let his eyes see his own calamity,
And let him from the Almighty's wrath have drink.

21. Since what cares he for his house after him,
When number of his months had been cut short ?

22. Can any one be teaching God to know
While He, yea He will judge exalted ones ?

23. This man may die in his perfected growth,
Wholly in his security and ease ;

24. His inward parts with fatness may be filled ;
And marrow may his bones be moistened with :

25. While that man dies with an embittered soul,
And never did he eat with mirthfulness.

26. Together on the dust they shall lie down,
And worms shall make a cover over them.

27. Lo ! I have known the projectings of you,
And violence of your designs at me ;

28. When ye say, "Where is house of noble-man?"
And "Where are tents in which the wicked dwelt?"

29. Have ye not asked the passers by the way ?
Also their signs will ye not recognise ?

30. Though at sore day may ill man be held back,
At day of raging they shall be led forth.

31. Who will expose before his face his way ?
And what he did, who will requite to him ?

32. Yet he himself shall to the graves be led,
And o'er the tomb shall be a wakeful watch.

33. Sweet unto him have clods of valley been ;
And on behind him shall all mankind draw,
As those before him have been numberless.

34. How then will ye give me vain comforting?
And your retorts have nothing left but wrong.

CHAPTER XXII.

1. THEN answered Eliphaz the Temanite, and said:
2. Can any strong man profit unto God
As wise-doer can profit other men?
3. Would the Almighty joy if thou wert just?
Or gain if thou wert perfecting thy ways?
4. Doth He against thy reverence check thee,
And enter into judgement with thyself?
5. Hath not thine evilness been manifold,
And thine iniquities been limitless?
6. For thou wouldst pledge thy brother needlessly;
And garments of the naked thou would'st strip.
7. No weary one got water drink from thee,
And thou from hungry one withheldest bread.
8. But man of arm, to him hath been the land;
And favoured personage hath sat therein.
9. The widows thou didst send forth emptily;
Also the arms of orphans would be crusht.
10. Therefore all round about thee have been traps,
And sorely trouble thee would sudden dread;
11. Or else a darkness that thou shouldst see nought;
And sweep of waters would o'ercover thee.
12. Is it not God who makes the heavens high?
See thou the starry host, how lifted up!
13. Yet thou wast saying, "What can God have known?"
"Through a thick cloud of darkness can He judge?"
14. "Thick clouds concealing Him, He can see nought;"
"And heaven's circle He will make His walk
15. Wouldst thou observe the old frequented path
On which the men of lawlessness have trod?
16. Those who had been arrested without time;

Like river their foundation would be poured :

17. Those saying unto God, "Depart from us,"
    And, "What can the Almighty do to them?"

18. Yet He it was who filled their homes with good.
    And wicked's counsel hath been far from me.

19. The righteous men shall see, and will be glad ;
    And man of innocence will mock at them.

20. "Surely our standing crop hath been kept hid ; "
    "But their full stock a fire hath eaten up."

21. O be acquaint with Him, and be in peace !
    Thereby may'st thou increasingly have good.

22. O be receiving from His mouth a law !
    And do thou put His sayings in thy heart !

23. Return to the Almighty ; be built up ;
    Far do thou keep injustice from thy tents :

24. And do thou put defence upon the dust,
    And Ophir mid the hard stone of the brooks ;

25. For the Almighty is thy full defence,
    And silver's piling quantities for thee.

26. For then thou in the Almighty wilt delight,
    And wilt be lifting toward God thy face :

27. Thou may'st intreat Him, and He will hear thee ;
    And thou may'st make performance of thy vows :

28. And what thou sayest shall stand firm for thee ;
    Also upon thy ways a light will shine.

29. When men bring low, then thou mayst say " Look
        up ; "
    And man of downcast eyes will He make safe.

30. He will keep free the land of innocent
    And it is freed by cleanness of thy hands.

CHAPTER XXIII.

1. THEN answered Job, and said ;
2. Even to-day 'tis bitter my complaint !

My hand weighs heavily upon my sigh !

3. O that I did know, and were finding Him !
   That I might enter even to His seat !

4. I would array in sight of Him the cause ;
   And I would fill my mouth with arguments.

5. I fain would know what He would answer me,
   And would discern what He would say to me,

6. Would He in His great strength contend with me ?
   Nay. Ah ! He would himself put into me.

7. Thus when uprightly reasoning with Him
   I fain would get full quittance from my Judge.

8. Lo ! forward I may go, but He is not ;
   And backward, but without perceiving Him ;

9. On left hand, while He works, I cannot gaze ;
   He shrouds the right hand, and I cannot see.

10. Yet He hath known the way which is with me ;
    He hath tried me, like gold shall I come forth

11. Upon His goings hath my foot kept hold ;
    His way I have observed, and would not slant.

12. His lips' commandments I will not remove ;
    In breast I store the sayings of His mouth.

13. But He is one, and who may turn Him back ?
    And what His soul desireth, He will do.

14. Surely He will perform my destiny ;
    And like these same things many are with Him.

15. Therefore at face of Him I troubled am ;
    When I consider, I have dread of Him.

16. Yea, God hath caused a softness of my heart ;
    And the Almighty hath sore troubled me ;

17. That I was not supprest before the dark ;
    Nor from my presence did He cover gloom.

CHAPTER XXIV.

1. WHY, from the Almighty have not times been stored?
    Nor have those knowing Him gazed on his days?
2. The marks of boundary they will remove;
    A flock they snatched away, that they may herd.
3. The ass of orphan children they lead off;
    They take the ox of widow for a pledge;
4. They turn the needy persons from the way;
    In groups are hid the meek ones of the land.
5. Behold! wild asses of the wilderness,
    They go to their work, early seeking prey;
    Mixture for him, and bread for the young lads.
6. Out in the field poor provender they reap;
    And vineyard of a wicked man they glean.
7. Each naked they will lodge without attire,
    So that there is no cover in the cold.
8. From downpour on the hills will they be wet,
    And without shelter they embrace the rock.
9. They will snatch off from breast the orphan child,
    And on a sufferer will force a pledge;
10. Each naked they must walk without attire,
    And hungry ones have borne away a sheaf:
11. Between the walls of these they make bright oil;
    They trod the presses, yet will suffer thirst:
12. Out from the city mortal men will groan,
    And soul of wounded men will cry for help,
    And God will not be laying foolishness.
13. They, they have been with rebels against light;
    They have not recognised the ways of it,
    Nor have been sitting in the paths of it.
14. At light-time will arise a murderer,
    Will kill the suffering and needy one,
    And in the night will he be as a thief.

15. And the adultrous eye hath watched the dusk,
Saying "There shall no eye be viewing me,"
And under secresy he puts his face.

16. One diggeth into houses in the dark;
Through daytime they have kept themselves sealed
up,
They have not known the light.

17. For always morning is to them deathshade;
For each discerns the terrors of deathshade.

18. Swift he will be upon the water's face;
Reviled shall be their portion in the earth;
He will not face the way of the vineyards.

19. A drought and also heat
Will catch away the waters of the snow;
They fatally have sinned.

20. The womb forgets him, worms are sweet on him;
No more is he in mind;
Injustice shall be broken like a tree.—

21. Shepherd of barren woman who bears not,
Also of widow to whom none doth good,

22. He hath been drawing great ones by His strength;
He riseth, and no man is sure of life.

23. It may be given him trustfully to lean;
But eyes of Him are on the ways of them.

24. High for a little, soon he is no more;
They fall down low; like all they are shut up;
And like a mass of corn-ears they are mown.

25. And surely now, who would cause me to lie?
And would be setting down at nought my speech?

CHAPTER XXV.

1. THEN answered Bildad the Shuhite, and said:

2. The sovran rule and dread must be with Him,
Who worketh peace in His exalted heights.

3. Can there be any number of His troops?
    And upon whom doth not His light arise?
4. But how shall feeble man be just with God?
    And how can one of woman born be pure?
5. Behold! the very moon! it could not shine,
    Nor have the stars been pure in sight of Him.
6. Much less then feeble man, who is a grub,
    And son of Adam, who is but a worm?

CHAPTER XXVI.

1. THEN answered Job, and said:
2. How hast thou holpen him who had not strength?
    Or didst thou save the arm which had not power?
3. How hast thou counselled him who is not wise?
    And made efficiency be amply known?
4. With whom hast thou been showing forth discourse?
    And breath of whom was issuing from thee?
5. The shady ghosts are being reproduced
    Beneath the seas and their inhabitants.
6. Naked must Sheol be in front of Him,
    Also Abaddon hath no covering.
7. He stretches out the north o'er empty space,
    And hangeth up the earth on no support:
8. He bindeth waters into His thick clouds,
    And thinner cloud is not cleft under them:
9. He keepeth shut the presence of His throne,
    And He hath spread a thin cloud over it;
10. A circle He decreed on water's face,
    Unto the very edge of light and dark.
11. The pillars of the heavens tremble shall,
    And they will be amazed at His rebuke.
12. He by His strength did quickly quell the sea,
    And by His skilfulness struck Rahab through.
13. His Spirit hath made heavens beautiful;

His head hath pierced the serpent fugitive.

14. Lo! these are outskirts of the ways of Him :
But what a little hint is heard thereby ;
And thunder of His might who comprehends ?

CHAPTER XXVII.

1. MOREOVER Job continued his parable, and said :
2. God ever-living took away my right,
And the Almighty gave me bitter soul.
3. Yet all the while my breath remains in me,
And God's own spirit in my nostril is,
4. My lips shall not speak anything unjust,
Nor shall my tongue be talking guilefully.
5. May God forbid my justifying you !
   Until I must expire,
I shall not put my perfectness from me.
6. Upon my righteousness I have kept hold,
   And will not let it go ;
My heart gives no reproaching from my days.
7. Like wicked man shall be mine enemy ;
And mine upriser like a man unjust.
8. For what is hypocrite's expectancy,
   Although he might make gain,
When God will surely take away his soul ?
9. Will God be listening to his outcry,
When trouble shall be coming in on him ?
10. If he in the Almighty do delight,
He ought to call on God at every time.
11. I would direct yourselves by hand of God ;
What the Almighty owns, I will not hide.
12. Lo! ye yourselves, yea all of you, have gazed ;
And why is this ? ye will be wholly vain.
13. Such portion hath a wicked man with God ;
   Also this heritage

From the Almighty, tyrants shall receive.

14. If his sons multiply, 'tis for the sword ;
His offspring shall not be sufficed with bread.

15. Those left of him shall buried be in death ;
Also his widowed women shall not weep.

16. Though he be heaping silver like as dust ;
And be preparing raiment like as clay ;

17. He may prepare, but righteous man shall wear ;
And silver shall an innocent partake.

18. He had been building like the moth his house,
And like the covert which a keeper makes.

19. Rich he lies down, but shall not gathered be ;
His eyes he opened, but he was no more.

20. Like waters, terrors are o'ertaking him ;
At night a tempest stealeth him away ;

21. An east wind lifteth him, and he must go ;
And it will wildly swirl him from his place.

22. And He will cast on him, and will not spare ;
From hand of Him he will in fleeing flee.

23. Each will be striking on themselves their palms,
And each will hiss upon him from his place.

CHAPTER XXVIII.

1. SURELY there is for silver an outlet ;
Also a place for gold, which men refine.

2. The iron from the dust is taken out,
Also the stone will pour out molten brass.

3. Man sets an end to dark,
And to the utmost will be searching out
The stone of gloominess and of deathshade.

4. Breaching a mine away from sojourning,
Those who have been forgotten from the foot
Have gone down low, from men have strolled away.

5. The earth, from out of it should come forth bread ;
But underneath, it has been turned like fire.

6. A place of sapphires are the stones of it,
   Also to it belong the dusts of gold.

7. A pathway which no bird of prey hath known,
   Nor hath the eye of vulture glared on it ;

8. The sons of fierceness have not trodden it ;
   Nor hath the jackal been frequenting it :

9. Against the flinty rock he sent his hand ;
   He overturned the mountains from the root :

10. He through the rocks hath cloven passages,
    And every precious thing his eye hath seen :

11. From trickling flow he hath dammed rivers up,
    And that which was held hid he brings to light.

12. But real wisdom, whence shall it be found ?
    And where may place be of intelligence ?

13. Frail man knows not the valuing of it,
    Nor is it found in land of living men.

14. The surging deep saith, " It is not in me ; "
    And sea hath said, " It is not about me."

15. A purse may not be given instead of it ;
    Nor may a weight of silver be its price :

16. It cannot be surpassed by Ophir's gold,
    By precious onyx, or by sapphire stone :

17. Nor gold nor crystal can bear rank with it ;
    Nor its exchange be vessels of fine gold.

18. Let pearls and coral not be kept in mind ;
    Yea, wisdom's gaining beyond rubies is.

19. It shall not rank with topazes of Cush ;
    By clean pure gold it cannot be surpassed.

20. But real wisdom, whence then will it come ?
    And where may place be of intelligence ?

21. Since hid it is from every living eye,
    And from the fowl of heaven it secret is.

22. Abaddon, also death themselves have said,
    " We with our ears have heard report of it."

23. Great God made way of it be understood ;

And He, yea He hath known the place of it.
24. For He, yea He to ends of earth would look,
   Beneath the whole of heaven He would see,
25. As to the making for the wind a weight,
   And waters He did mete with measurement,
26. When He was making for the rain a law,
   Also a way for bolts of thunderings.
27. Then did He see it, and would tell it forth ;
   Did stablish it ; yea, He did search it out.
28.　　　And He to mankind saith,
   " Lo ! fearing the great Lord is wisdom true,
   " And shunning evil is intelligence."

CHAPTER XXIX.

1. MOREOVER Job continued his parable, and said ;
2. O that I might be as in months gone past !
   As in the days when God was keeping me !
3. When shining was His lamp upon my head,
   By His own light could I walk through the dark :
4. Such as I had been in my days of prime,
   When secret love of God was on my tent :
5. While there was yet the Almighty One with me,
   And round about me were my growing youths :
6. When washed with butter had my goings been,
   And rock would pour about me rills of oil.
7. As I went outward to the city gate,
   In the broad place I would prepare my seat,
8. The young men saw me, and did hide themselves,
   And very aged men uprising stood :
9. The princes did refrain in argument,
   And they would put their palm upon their mouth :
10. The voices of the leading men were hid ;
   Also their tongue did to their palate cling.
11. When ear did hear, it hailed my happiness ;

Or eye did see, it witness bore of me,

12. That I would free a sufferer who cried,
Also a fatherless who had no help.

13. Blessing of perishing would come to me,
And heart of widow I would cause to cheer.

14. I put on righteousness, and me it clothed ;
As robe and turban did my judgement fit.

15. As eyes did I become unto the blind,
And feet unto the crippled one was I :

16. A father I was unto needy folks ;
And strife, which I knew not, I would search thro':

17. And I would break the fangs of unjust man,
And from his teeth I would cast out the prey.

18. And said that with my nest I would expire,
And like the sand I would increase my days.

19. My root toward the waters be outspread,
And dew would lodge among my tender shoots.

20. My glory would continue fresh with me,
Also my bow would in my hand improve.

21. For me men listened, and did hopeful wait,
And would with stillness take my counselling :

22. After my words they would not speak again,
But upon them my argument would drop ;

23. They looked with hope like rainseekers to me,
And gaped their mouth as for the latter rain.

24. I might laugh at them, they might not believe ;
But light of my face they would not let fall.

25. I would choose out their way, and would sit chief ;
And I would dwell as king among the troop ;
Also like one who comforts them who mourn.

CHAPTER XXX.

1. BUT now ! there have been laughing against me,
Those who are greatly younger than myself,

Although I did reject their forefathers
To act along with dogs of my sheepfold.

2. Yea, what would strength of their hands do for me,
When on themselves hath fitness become lost?

3. In want and in depressing dreariness,
      They range through the dry land
Already ruinous and desolate;

4. Those who do crop off mallows by the bush,
And take the root of junipers for food.

5. They from society are driven out;
Men will raise shout against them as a thief;

6. In frightful places of ravines to dwell,
The holes of earth, and cavities of rock:

7. Among the bushes they are wont to bray,
Beneath the nettles they are wont to meet;

8. The sons of fool, yea sons without a name;
      They have been broken from the earth.

9. And now, the song of these men I have been,
And I must be to these men for a talk.

10. They have abhorred me, have kept far from me,
And from my face have not withheld their spit.

11. Since he his cord let loose, and humbleth me,
The bridle from before me they have sent.

12. At the right hand an upstart brood will rise;
      My feet they have sent off;
And raise against me their destructive paths.

13.   They have broke down my road;
My sore distressedness they will promote,
      No helper is to them.

14. Like a wide-spreading breach they will arrive;
Beneath the wreckage they have rolled themselves.

15. The turning down on me of terrorings,
Pursuing like the wind my nobleness;
And like thick cloud my safety hath passed off.

16. And now! on me my soul will pour itself;

Days of affliction will keep hold of me.

17. At night my bones He hath picked off from me ;
   Also my shifting pains will not lie down.

18. With much strength will my clothing be disguised ;
   Like collar of my coat it girdeth me.

19.   He hath shot me to clay,
   And I must class myself with dust and ash.

20. I cry to Thee, but Thou wilt not reply ;
   While I have stood, Thou wouldst consider me.

21. Thou turnest to be cruel unto me ;
   With Thy strong hand Thou art opposing me ;

22. Wilt lift me to the wind, wilt make me ride,
   And Thou wilt melt me most effectively.

23. For I do know that death will take me back,
   Also the house where all who live shall meet.

24. Ah ! at no ruin will He send a hand,
   If in his damage there be cry for grace.

25. Surely I did weep at a troublous day ;
   My soul did sorrow for the needy man.

26. Though good I did expect, yet evil comes ;
   And I would hope for light, yet here comes gloom.

27. My bowels boiling were, and did not calm ;
   Days of affliction have confronted me.

28. In mourning I have gone without the sun,
   I rose, in congregation I cried help.

29. A brother I have been to noxious beasts,
   And a companion to the howling birds.

30. My skin was early seeking off from me,
   Also my bones were kindling with dry heat.

31. So that my harp is turned to mournfulness,
   Also my pipe to voice of them who weep.

CHAPTER XXXI.

1. A COVENANT I did make for mine eyes,
   And what regard to virgin should I give?
2. And what is portion from the God above,
   And heritage from Mighty One on high?
3. Is not calamity for unjust man,
   And wrath for them who act ungodliness?
4. Is it not He, yea He who sees my ways,
   And doth of all my footsteps take account?
5. If I have walked along with worthlessness,
   Or if my foot would hasten to deceit;
6. Let Him weigh me in scales of righteousness,
   And God will know mine own integrity.
7. If slanting was my going from the way;
   And following mine eye my heart would walk;
   Or to my palm were clinging any blot;
8. Though I might sow, yet would another eat,
   And mine own offspring would be rooted out.
9. If my heart had been lured by womankind,
   And at my neighbour's entrance I laid wait,
10. Then let my wife grind for another man,
    And upon her let others bow themselves.
11.   For that were heinous crime;
    And such iniquity must be condemned.
12. Yea, it is fire which to Abaddon eats,
    And into all mine increase it would root.
13. If I reject the right of serving-man,
    Or serving-maid when they contend with me,
14. What then could I do when God riseth up?
    And when he visits what could I charge back?
15. Did not my Maker in the womb make him?
    And was not One our Framer before birth?
16. If I withheld poor people from delight,

Or if I caused a widow's eyes to fail;

17. Or I would eat my morsel all alone,
So that no fatherless did eat thereof;

18. Though from my youth he reared me fatherlike,
And from my birth I ought to be her guide:

19. If I should see one swooning without clothes,
Or needy one who had no covering;

20. If such one's loins had not been blessing me,
Nor from my lamb's fleece could he warm himself;

21. If I did shake my hand at fatherless,
When in the gateway I could see my help;

22. Then let my shoulder fall from collar-bone,
And let mine arm be broken from its shank.

23. For dread to me is God's calamity,
And from His dignity I could do nought.—

24. If I were making gold my confidence,
Or to pure gold have said, " My trust art thou ; "

25. If I would gladden when my wealth increased,
And when my hand had found abundantly;

26. If I would see the light when it did shine,
Or else the moon in brilliance moving on,

27. And secretly my heart would be allured,
So that my hand gave kissing to my mouth;

28. This too would be condemned iniquity,
Because I had denied the God above.—

29. If at my hater's damage I was glad,
And roused myself when evil found him out,

30. I did not let my palate sin so far
As asking with a curse the soul of him.

31. Surely the inmates of my tent did say,
" Give of his flesh, we are not satisfied ; "

32. In outfield would no sojourner be lodged;
My doors I to the wayfarer would ope.—

33. If I did cover, Adam-like, my sins,
Hiding in close place mine iniquity;

34. Because I feared a multitude grown great,
Or families' contempt would break me down ;
And keeping still, I went not out of doors :

35. Oh ! that I had one listening to me !
Behold my plea ! Almighty, answer me,
And book which man who striveth with me wrote !

36. Surely on shoulder I would carry it,
Would tie it as a crowning for myself.

37. The number of my steps I would show Him ;
I as a leader would go near to Him.

38. If against me my ground were crying out,
And if together will its furrows weep ;

39. If strength thereof I did eat without pay,
Or forced its holders to breathe out their soul ;

40. Instead of wheat let there be growing thorns ;
Also instead of barley noxious weeds.
The words of Job are ended.

CHAPTER XXXII.

1. So these three men ceased to answer Job, because
he was righteous in his own eyes. 2. Then would kindle
the anger of Elishu, son of Barachel the Buzite, of the
family of Ram ; against Job did his anger kindle because
he justified his own soul more than great God. 3. Also
against his three friends did his anger kindle, because
they had found no answer by which they might condemn
Job. 4. And Elihu had earnestly waited for Job with
words, because they were older then he. 5. But when
Elihu saw that there was no answer in the mouth of these
three men, then his anger would kindle. 6. And Elihu,
son of Barachel the Buzite, answered and said ;

I am but short of days, and you quite old ;
Therefore have I been shy :
Fearing to make my knowledge plain with you.

7. I had been saying, days are what should speak,
   And multitude of years make wisdom known.
8. Nevertheless That spirit dwells in man,
   And breath Almighty makes them understand.
9.   Not many may be wise ;
   Nor may old men be competent to judge.
10. Therefore I said, O listen thou to me !
    I will make plain my knowledge, even I.
11. Lo ! I did hopefully wait for your words ;
    I long gave ear for your skilled arguments,
    Until ye might have searched out what to say.
12. And unto you I would give full regard ;
    But lo ! there was no one convincing Job,
    No answer to his sayings from yourselves.
13. Lest ye should say, " We have found wisdom out,
    God must be tossing him ; it is not man."
14. But he hath not arrayed to me a speech ;
    Nor with your sayings will I charge him back.
15. They were cast down ; they did not answer more :
    They have put from them further argument.
16. So I was hoping, but they will not speak ;
    Though they have stood, they do not answer more.
17. I will give answer, even I, my part ;
    I will make plain my knowledge, even I.
18.   For I am full of speech ;
    The spirit of my belly urgeth me.
19. Behold ! my belly is like wine pent up ;
    Like bottles which are new, it will be burst.
20. I shall be speaking, and will breathe myself ;
    Will ope my lips, and will be answering.
21. O let me not lift up the face of man,
    Nor to mankind shall I be using names ;
22. When I know nothing about using names,
    Some little may my Maker lift up me.

CHAPTER XXXIII.

1. WHEREFORE, O Job, pray listen to my speech !
   And unto all my words do thou give ear.

2. Behold, I pray you ! since I ope my mouth,
   My tongue hath with my palate spoken out.

3. Uprightness of my heart my sayings prove :
   And knowledge have my lips most clearly told.

4. The spirit of the mighty God made me,
   And breath of the Almighty gives me life.

5. If thou be able, do thou charge me back ;
   Array before me ; do thou take thy stand.

6. Lo ! I, like thine own mouth, belong to God ;
   From clay have I been moulded, also I.

7. Behold ! my terror will not frighten thee ;
   Nor shall my palm be heavy upon thee.

8. Ah ! thou wast saying in the ear of me,
   And voice of speechifying I could hear ;

9. " Quite pure am I, and without trespassing ;
   Quite safe am I, with no iniquity.

10. Lo ! quarrellings against me He would find ;
    And thinketh me an enemy to Him.

11. He will be putting in the stocks my feet,
    And he will be observing all my paths."

12. Lo ! there thou wert not just ; I answer thee,
    That greater must be God than feeble man.

13. Now wherefore toward Him didst thou contend
    That all His matters He will not explain ?

14. Although at one occasion God may speak,
    And at a second, He may view it not ;

15. During a dream, a vision of the night,
    When falls a deep sleep upon feeble men,
    During the slumberings upon the bed,

16. Then He unveils the ear of feeble men,

And He the discipline of them will seal,

17. To turn aside mankind from what they do ;
    And pride from strong man He will cover up.
18. He will keep back the soul of him from ditch,
    Also his life from passing off by dart :
19. While checked is he with pain upon his bed,
    And striving of his bones hath been severe ;
20. So that his life was nauseating bread,
    Also his soul the food he should desire ;
21. Failing would be his flesh from sightliness,
    And bones which were not seen grew prominent :
22. And near unto the ditch his soul would draw,
    Also his life unto the grips of death.
23. If truly with him be a messenger,
    One of a thousand, an interpreter,
    To show to any man his uprightness ;
24. Then He will treat him graciously, and say,
    " Redeem thou him from going down to ditch,
        I having found a ransom."
25. More healthy shall his flesh be than a child's ;
    He shall return to days of youthfulness :
26. He pleads to God, and He will favour him,
    And he shall see His face with joyful shout ;
    And He restores to man his righteousness.
27. He sings beside frail men, and he will say,
    " While I did sin, and was perverting right,
        " It nought availed for me ;
28. " He hath redeemed my soul from way of ditch,
    " Also my life shall see into the light."
29. Lo ! all these things the mighty God will do
    Times oft and plenteously with man of strength,
30. So to bring back the soul of him from ditch,
    To be enlit with light of living men.
31. Be heedful, Job ! O listen thou to me :
    Stand thou aloof ; and I myself will speak.

32. If truly there be speech, then charge me back ;
    Speak thou, for fain would I esteem thee just.
33. If naught to say, then listen thou to me ;
    Stand thou aloof, while wisely I train thee.

CHAPTER XXXIV.

1. So Elihu was answering, and said ;
2. Do ye be hearing, O wise men, my speech ;
   And knowing men, do ye give ear to me.
3. Because the ear is trier of discourse,
   And palate will be taster of its food.
4. Judgement let us be choosing for ourselves,
   Let us know well among us what is good.
5. For Job hath said, " I did act righteously,
   But mighty God did take away my right.
6. About my right I might be telling lies ;
   Sore is my shaft-wound without trespass-cause."
7.   What strong man is like Job ?
   He will drink mockery like water draft.
8. He clubs with actors of ungodliness,
   And walks along with men of wickedness.
9. For he hath said, strong man will profit naught
   By being in acceptance with great God.
10. Therefore, O men of heart, list ye to me ;
    Afar from God be any wicked act,
    From the Almighty any act unjust !
11. For mankind's work He will requite to each,
    And like our path, so He will make us find.
12. Yea, truly, God will not cause wickedness,
    Nor will the Almighty be perverting right.
13. Who did commit to him the forming earth ?
    And who set all the habitable world ?
14. Were He to set toward Himself His heart,
    Or gather up His spirit and His breath,

15. Expiring would all flesh together be,
    And mankind on the dust would lie again.
16. But if thou understandest, hear thou this ;
    Do thou give ear to voice of my discourse !
17. Yea, is a judgement-hater fit to rule ?
    Or the most Righteous One wilt thou condemn ?
18. Even Him who saith to any worthless king,
        One wicked toward nobles,
19. That He respecteth not the face of prince,
    Nor doth acknowledge wealthy before poor,
    Because they all are His own handiwork ?
20. In moment they may die, and at midnight ;
    A folk are heaved, and they will pass away ;
    A mighty one departs, though not by hand.
21. For eyes of Him are on the ways of man,
    And all the steps of each one He will see.
22. There is not any darkness or deathshade
    Where actors of ungodliness may hide.
23. Surely on no man need He further lay
    That toward God in judgement he must go.
24. He will be blighting strong men beyond search,
    And will make others stand instead of them.
25. Therefore He notes the servitudes of them ;
    And overthrows at night, and they are crusht.
26. As being wicked He hath stricken them,
        Where men are seeing them ;
27. Because they turned from following of Him,
    And all His ways they would not wisely learn :
28. Bringing on Him the outcry of the poor,
    And outcries of afflicted He will hear.
29. If He, yea He give stillness, who can harm ?
    And when He hides His face, who can view Him ?
    Whether on nation or on man alike ;
30. That neither hypocritic man may reign,
        Nor people be ensnared.

31. Surely to mighty God it may be said,
    " I have been bearing ; I would not be vain ;
32. " Beyond my gaze be Thou, Thou pointing me ;
    " Unjustly I did act ; I will not add."
33. Is it by thy mind that He must requite,
        Although thou didst reject ?
    For thou, yea thou art chooser, and not I ;
    And what thou hast been knowing do thou speak.
34. The men of heartfulness will say to me,
    And man of wisdom listening to me ;
35. " Job not with proper knowledge would speak on,
    " Nor had his words a good instructiveness."
36. I would that Job be tested thoroughly
    About retorts with men of godlessness.
37. For on his sin he will add trespassing ;
        Among us he will strike,
    And multiply his sayings about God.

CHAPTER XXXV.

1. AND Elihu was answering, and said :
2. Is this thy reckoning of judgement just ?
   Thou saidst, " My righteousness doth come from
       God ? "
3. Yet thou wilt say, " What doth it profit thee ?
   What usefulness may I get from my sin ?"
4. I will, yea I will charge thee back in speech,
   And thy companions along with thee.
5. Be looking to the heavens, and see thou ;
   And view the skies, how high they are from thee.
6. If sinful thou, what dost thou against Him ?
   What with much trespass couldst thou do to Him
7. If righteous thou, what canst thou give to Him ?
   Or what from hand of thee would He receive ?
8. To man like thyself be thy wickedness,

To son of Adam be thy righteousness.

9. From oft oppressions they are crying out ;
   They cry for help from arm of many men.
10. But none saith, " Where may God my maker be ? "
    Who giveth tuneful hymnings in the night ;
11. Who traineth us beyond the beasts of earth,
    And more than fowls of heaven makes us wise.
12. There they cry out, but no one answereth
    Because of the proud bearing of ill men.
13. Ah ! worthlessness God will not listen to,
    Nor will the Almighty be regarding it.
14. Yea, though thou say, thou getst no view of Him,
    Plead thou before Him, and be stayed to Him.
15. But now because His anger visits not,
    And into fault He hath not closely known ;
16. Job will be vainly opening his mouth,
    In lack of knowledge he will strengthen speech.

CHAPTER XXXVI.

1. THEN Elihu was adding, and he said ;
2. Be with me shortly, till I show to thee
   That yet for God there may be things to say.
3. I will lift up my knowledge to afar ;
   And to my Maker will give righteousness.
4. For verily not false will be my speech ;
   The perfectness of knowledge is with thee.
5. Lo ! God is mighty, and will not reject ;
   Mighty is He of strength of heart.
6. He will not keep alive a wicked man ;
   But judgement of the meek ones He will give.
7. He holds not off from righteous man His eyes,
   But near enthroned kings
   He seats them firmly, and they shall be high.
8. But if they, being bound in fetterings,

May have been caught in cords of suffering,
9. Then He will manifest to them their acts,
   And their transgressions when they bragged them-
     selves ;
10. He will unveil their ear to discipline,
    And say, they must return from godlessness.
11. If they will be obedient, and will serve,
    They shall complete their days in mirthfulness,
    Also their years in ample pleasantness.
12. If disobedient, they by shaft shall pass,
    And they in lack of knowledge shall expire.
13. And hypocritic hearts move angriness ;
    They will not cry for help when He binds them.
14. Dying in very youth their soul shall be ;
    Also their life shall be with the unclean.
15. He pulls meek man through his afflictedness,
    And through oppression He unveils their ear.
16. Yea, He did urge thyself from mouth of strait,
    Widely, where is no anguish underneath ;
    And thine own table would be fatly filled.
17. But plea of wicked man thou hast filled up ;
    The plea and judgment will be keeping hold.
18. Yea these, lest He should urge thee with a stroke
    And a great ransom might not make thee turn.
19. Will He compare thy wealth? not with distress,
    And all the masterfulnesses of strength.
20. O may'st not thou be panting for the night,
    For upgoing of peoples under them.
21. Do thou keep watch, turn not to godlessness ;
    For that, more than affliction, was thy choice.
22. Lo! God exalts to safety by His strength ;
    Who can be a director such as He?
23. Who hath appointed unto Him his way?
    Or who saith, "Thou hast done what is unjust ?"
24. Remember that thou magnify His act,

That which frail men have diligently sung ;
25. The whole of humankind have gazed on it ;
Frail man will be on-looking from afar.
26. Lo ! God is great beyond what we can know ;
Of His repeated acts there is no search.
27. For He will draw away the water-drops ;
They will refine the rain to mist thereof ;
28. That which will be down-flowing from the skies,
Will be distilled on man abundantly.
29. Yea, let him mark the spreadings of thick cloud,
The crashing roars of His pavilion ;
30. Lo ! He hath spread out over it His light ;
And He the roots of sea hath covered up.
31. Because by these He will redress the folks ;
He also will give food in plenteousness.
32. To right and left He hath o'ercovered light,
And layeth charge on it to intercede :
33. Declaring as to Him will be His shout ;
The cattle even as to who comes up !

CHAPTER XXXVII.

1. YEA, and at this my heart goes tremblingly,
And will be moving loosely from its place.
2. Hear ye, O hear the rumbling of His voice !
And muttering which from His mouth will go !
3. Beneath all heavens He directeth it,
Also His light to outskirts of the earth.
4. And after it there will out-roar a voice ;
He thunders with His voice of majesty,
And will not stop them though His voice be heard.
5. God thundereth with His voice wondrously,
Outworking great things which we do not know.
6. For to the snow He saith, " Be thou on earth ; "
And heavy shower of rain,

And heavy shower of rainings of His strength.

7. The hand of all mankind He will seal up,
   That all frail men whom He hath made may know :

8. And animals will go to lurking place,
   And in their chosen lairs they will abide.

9. Out from the chamber will a tempest come,
   And from the scattering winds a freezing cold.

10. From breath of mighty God is given ice ;
    And width of waters is in hard restraint.

11. Yea, He with moisture loadeth a thick cloud ;
    A thin cloud will be scattered by His light :

12. And He on every side doth turn Himself,
    With combinations for their acting out
    Whatever He may be commanding them
    Upon the face of habitable earth ;

13. Whether it be for rod, or for his earth,
    Or for a mercy which He makes it find.

14. Do thou be giving ear to this, O Job !
    Stand, and consider wondrous works of God.

15. Can'st thou know how God layeth upon them ?
    And shineth forth the light of His thin cloud ?

16. Can'st thou know all the rollings of thick cloud,
    The wondrous works of perfect knowingness ?

17. That which doth cause thy garments to be hot
    When earth gets restful stillness from the south.

18. Canst thou with Him make an expanded sky
    As firm as is a molten looking-glass ?

19. Make thou us know what we should say to Him ;
    In face of darkness we cannot array.

20. Shall it be told to Him that I would speak ?
    If man say aught, he might be swallowed up.

21. But now although they have not seen the light,
    Most brilliant it must be amid the skies ;
    And wind doth pass, and will be cleansing them.

22. Out of the north gold splendour will arrive ;

On God there is a fearful majesty !

23. Almighty One, we have not found out Him,
      Most great of strength and judgement He must be ;
      And very righteous ; He will not afflict.

24. Therefore have feeble men a fear of Him ;
      He sees not any to be wise in heart.

CHAPTER XXXVIII.

1. THEN would Jehovah answer Job from the whirl-
wind, and say ;

2. Who may be this man making counsel dark
            By speeches without knowledge ?

3. Do thou be girding like strong man thy loins ;
      As I will ask thee, do thou make me know.

4. Where mightst thou be when I did found the earth ?
      Declare if thou hast known intelligence.

5. Who set its measurings, if thou mayst know ?
      Or who did stretch out over it a line ?

6. Down upon what were sunk its sockettings ?
      Or who did lay the cornerstone thereof ?

7. While sang in company the stars of morn,
      And joyful shouted all the sons of God.

8. And He closed in with double doors the sea,
      When bursting, it would issue from the womb ;

9. When I did set thin cloud for clothing it,
      And awful gloom to be enswaddling it ;

10. And I was breaking out its destined range,
      And would be setting bar and double doors ;

11. And I was saying, " Hereto thou mayst come,
            But not beyond,
      For this shall stand against thy proudest waves."

12. Hast thou from thy days had command of morn ?
      Hast thou been causing dawn to know its place ?

13. For catching hold on outskirts of the earth,

And wicked men shall be tossed out from it.

14. It turns itself like clay to be ensealed ;
    And they will take their stand as if full clad.

15. Whereas withheld from wicked is their light,
    And arm which is exalted shall be broke.

16. Hast thou explored into the springs of sea?
    Or walked about in search of surging deep?

17. Were gates of death made manifest to thee?
    And wouldst thou see the gateways of deathshade?

18. Hast thou considered well the breadths of earth?
    Declare if thou hast known the whole of it.

19. Which is the way to where the light doth dwell?
    And darkness, where may be the place for it?

20. That thou mayst take it to its boundary,
    And mayst discern the pathways of its house.

21. Thou knowest, because then thou wouldst be born,
    And number of thy days is manifold.

22. Hast thou gone in to treasuries of snow?
    And treasuries of hail mayst thou have seen?

23. Those which I keep against a troublous time,
    Against a day of conflict and of war.

24. Which is the way how light is portioned out?
    How east-wind scattereth upon the earth?

25. Who did divide for water-flood a trough ;
    Also a way for bolts of thunderings?

26. To cause a raining upon earth, not man ;
    A wilderness where none of mankind be ;

27. To satisfy the waste and desolate ;
    And to cause springing of the coming herbs.

28. Is there a real father to the rain?
    Or who begat the gatherings of dew?

29. Out of what belly did come forth the ice?
    And heaven's hoarfrost, who did give it birth?

30. Like to a stone the waters hide themselves ;
    And faces of the deep will catch themselves.

31. Dost thou bind close the ties of Pleiades,
    Or long cords of Orion dost thou loose?

32. Dost thou at due time bring out Mazzaroth?
    Or dost thou guide the Great Bear with her cubs?

33. Are heaven's ordinances known to thee,
    Yea, wilt thou set its ruling in the earth?

34. Wilt thou raise up to the thick cloud thy voice,
    So that sufficient waters cover thee?

35. Canst thou send lightnings forth, and will they go,
    While saying unto thee, " Lo ! here are we "?

36. Who did put wisdom in the private parts?
    Or give intelligence to secret force?

37. Who doth in wisdom numerate the skies?
    Or cause the jars of heaven to lie down,

38. When dust is being fused to solidness,
    Also the clods will be together joined?

39. Dost thou hunt down a prey for lioness,
    Or life of younger lions wilt thou fill?

40. While they will bow down in their chosen lairs,
    Will sit in covert as their lurking place,

41. Who doth provide the raven in its hunt?
    When its young brood to God will cry for help,
    They will be wandering for want of food.

CHAPTER XXXIX.

1. KNOWST thou the breeding time of mountain goats?
   The calving of the hinds wilt thou observe?

2. Wilt thou count out the months they should fill up?
   And hast thou known her time of giving birth?

3. They will bend down; their brood they will discharge;
   Their pangs they will completely send away.

4. Their young ones thrive; they will grow up with corn;

They have gone forth, and not returned to them.

5. Who hath sent out the wild ass to be free?
And bindings of the swift ass who hath loosed?

6. For whom I made the desert plain a home,
Also his dwelling place the land of salt:

7. He laugheth at the city's crowded stir;
A driver's blusterings he will not hear:

8. The range of mountains is his pasture ground,
And after every green thing he will seek.—

9. Will the wild bull consent to serving thee?
Will he indeed be lodging at thy crib?

10. Wilt thou bind that wild bull to furrow's rope?
Or will he harrow deep dales after thee?

11. Wilt thou trust him because his strength is great?
Or wilt thou leave to him thy labourage?

12. Wilt thou believe that he will come again
To gather in thy seed and threshing floor?—

13. The ostriches have an exultant wing
Of strength, of helpfulness, and showiness;

14. But she will leave upon the earth her eggs,
And on the dust she will be warming them;

15. Forgetting that a foot may injure it,
Or creature of the field may dash it out:

16. Her products are made hard, as not for her;
Un-needed is her labour, without dread;

17. Though God hath dealt her wisdom scantily,
Nor hath endowed her with intelligence,

18. What time aloft she will raise up herself,
At horse and at its rider she will laugh.—

19. Dost thou give to the horse his mightiness?
Dost thou clothe neck of him in thundriness?

20. Dost thou cause him to rush like locust swarm?
The grandeur of his snort is terrible.

21. They paw in the deep dale; he joys in strength;
He will go forth to meet the clash of arms:

22. He laughs at dread, and will not be cast down ;
     And will not turn aback from face of sword.

23. Upon him rattling will the quiver be,
     The flash of spearhead, and of javelin.

24. With rushing eagerness he skims the earth ;
     Nor will believe it is the trumpet voice.

25. While blares the trumpet, he will say, " Aha ! "
     And from afar will smell the battle's brunt,
     The thunder of the captains and the shout.—

26. Is it by thy mind that the hawk flies long,
     While spreading out its wings toward the south ?

27. Or at thy word will eagle soar on high,
                  And even raise his nest ?

28. On crag will dwell, and there will lodge himself
     On jutting of a crag and fortalice ?

29.   From whence he searcheth food ;
     To far off places will his eyes look out ;

30. Also his tender brood will suck up blood,
     And wheresoe'er the slain are, there is he.

CHAPTER XL.

1. THEN would Jehovah answer Job, and say ;

2. Will striving with the Almighty be put off ?
   Will challenger of God now answer this ?

3. And Job, as answering Jehovah, said ;

4. Lo ! I feel mean ; what can I charge Thee back ?
   My hand I must be laying on my mouth.

5. Once I did speak, but I could answer nought ;
   Yea, other times, but I will add no more.

6. Then would Jehovah answer Job from the whirl-
        wind, and say ;

7. Do thou be girding like strong man thy loins ;
   As I will ask thee, do thou make Me know.

8. Yea, wouldst thou cause My judgment to be void ?

Wilt thou condemn Me, that thou mayst be just?

9. Doth arm like that of God belong to thee?
   And canst thou thunder with a voice like His?

10. Bedeck thee now with pride and loftiness ;
    In splendid majesty clothe thou thyself ;

11. Scatter the outbursts of thine angriness ;
    And see each proud man, and bring thou him low ;

12. Seeing each proud man, him do thou subdue ;
    And drive the wicked men beneath themselves ;

13. Do thou hide them together in the dust ;
    Their faces do thou wrap in hiddenness.

14. And then might I, yea I be thanking thee,
    That thine own right hand could be saving thee.

15.   Behold now ! Behemoth,
    A creature which I made along with thee ;
    Of grasses like the oxen he will eat.

16. Behold now ! that his strength is in his loins,
    Also his vigour in his belly's nerve.

17. He will disport his trunk like cedar-tree ;
    The sinews of its dread will intertwine.

18. His body-parts are brazen channelings ;
    His bones are like to iron implements.

19. He is beginning of the ways of God ;
    The Maker of him will bring nigh his sword.

20. Sure feeding will the mountains yield to him ;
    And all the beasts of field will play thereon.

21. Beneath the lotus trees he will lie down ;
    In secresy of reeds and miry ground.

22. O'ercover him do lotus trees for shade ;
    Surrounding him are willows of the brook.

23. Lo ! river-flood may press, he hastes not off ;
               He will be confident
    Although a Jordan burst toward his mouth ;

24. He with his eyes will be receiving it ;
    He into snares will penetrate his nose.

CHAPTER XLI.

1. CANST thou draw out Leviathan with hook?
   Or with a cord canst thou subject his tongue?
2. Wilt thou insert a bulrush at his nose?
   Or with a thorn canst thou bore through his jaw?
3. Will he abound in supplicating thee?
   Even in speaking soft things unto thee?
4. Will he be making covenant with thee?
   Wilt thou take him for service lastingly?
5. Wilt thou make play with him as little bird?
   Or wilt thou bind him for thy younger maids?
6. Will companies be bargaining o'er him?
   Will they divide him among merchantmen?
7. Couldst thou with . . . fill the skin of him?
   Or with a . . . of fish the head of him?
8.   Lay thou on him thy palm;
   Remember thou the battle; add no more.
9. Behold! the hope of him hath been belied;
   Shall man from merest sight of him be cast?
10. None is so fierce that he will rouse up him;
    Who then before My face will take his stand?
11. Who did first bring me what I must requite?
    Beneath the whole of heaven all is Mine.
12. I will not leave his parts unspoken of,
    Also his might, and fit proportioning.
13. Who hath revealed the face of his attire?
    Or with his double bridle who will come?
14. The doors of his face who hath opened up?
    Around about his teeth are terrible.
15. A pride are the strong channelings of shields,
          Shut up with a close seal;
16. One with another they are set so near
    As that no air between them can come in.

17. Each to its neighbour will be so conjoined,
    They catch together, and will not go loose.
18. His neesing will cause shining of a light ;
    And his eyes are like eyelids of a dawn.
19. Out of his mouth will flaming torches go,
    And sparks of fire are making their escape.
20. Out of his nostrils there will issue smoke
    As of a steaming pot and bulrushes.
21. His breath will set the very coals ablaze ;
    Also a flame will from his mouth proceed.
22. In neck of him there will be lodging power,
    And at his presence . . .
23. The outflakes of his flesh together cling
    So firmly on him, it will not be moved.
24. The heart of him is firm as is a stone,
    Yea, firm as is a nether grinding slab.
25. From his uplifting will the strong men shrink
    From breakings they will try to clear themselves.
26. O'ertaking him the sword shall not arise,
    The spear, the missile, nor the coat of mail.
27. He will consider iron as but straw,
    And brass as but a wood of rottenness.
28. He will not be made flee by shaft of bow,
    To stubble have slingstones been turned for him ;
29. Like stubble too he hath considered clubs,
    And he will laugh at rushing javelin.
30. His underparts are sherds of earthenware ;
    He spreads a pointed harrow on the mud.
31. He sets the dark deep boiling like a pot;
    The sea he makes like a compounding mess.
32. Behind him he will cause a lighted path ;
    One might suppose the surging deep grown grey.
33. There is not on the dust the like of him,
    Who hath been made as not to be cast down.
34. Whatever thing is lofty he will see ;
    O'er all the sons of fierceness he is king.

CHAPTER XLII.

1. AND Job, as answering Jehovah, said ;
2. I know that Thou art able for the whole,
   And no design can be restrained from Thee.
3. What man is this who maketh counsel dim
   >In lack of knowledge ?
   Thus did I show what I could not discern,
   Things wondrously beyond what I could know.
4. O do Thou listen ! and I, I will speak ;
   I will ask Thee, and do Thou make me know.
5. With hearing of the ear I did hear Thee,
   But now it is mine eye which seeth Thee.
6. Wherefore I will reject, and do repent
   >Upon the dust and ashes.

7. And it was so, that after Jehovah had spoken these words unto Job, Jehovah would say unto Eliphaz the Temanite, "My anger is kindled against thee, and against thy two friends, for ye have not spoken of Me properly, as My servant Job. (8.) So now take for yourselves seven bullocks and seven rams, and go ye to My servant Job, and offer ye up a burnt offering for yourselves, and Job My servant shall pray for you, for his presence I will accept ; that there may be with you no working foolishly ; for ye did not speak of Me properly, as My servant Job." (9.) Then went Eliphaz the Temanite, and Bildad the Shuhite, and Zophar the Naamathite, and did according as Jehovah had said to them ; and Jehovah accepted the face of Job. (10.) And Jehovah turned back the captivity of Job when he prayed for his friends ; also Jehovah added to Job double of all which he had before. (11.) And then came to him all his brethren and all his sisters, and all his former acquaintances, and they did eat bread with him in

his house, and would condole with him, and comfort
him about all the evil which Jehovah had caused to
come on him; and they gave to him each man one
piece of money, and each man one earring of gold.
(12.) So Jehovah did bless the latter end of Job more
than his beginning: for he had fourteen thousand sheep,
and six thousand camels, and a thousand yoke of oxen,
and a thousand asses.   (13.) He had also seven sons and
three daughters.   (14.) And he called the name of the
first, Jemima; and the name of the second, Kezia; and
the name of the third, Keren-happuch.   (15.) And there
were not found any women so fair as the daughters of
Job in all the land; and their father gave to them in-
heritance among their brethren.   (16.) And Job lived
after this one hundred and forty years; and saw his sons,
and his sons' sons of four generations.   (17.) Then Job
died, being old, and full of days.

Of the alterations attention may be called to the following :—
vi. 6 ; xiii. 15 ; xiv. 19 ; xix. 26, 27 ; xxvi. 5 ; xxviii. 4, &c.;
xxx. 17 and 24 ; xxxiv. 18 ; xxxix. 13.

THE SONG OF SOLOMON.

THE SONG OF SOLOMON.

CHAPTER I.

1. THE Song of Songs, which is Solomon's,
2.   *She.* Let him kiss me with kisses of his mouth;
For good be thy endearments more than wine.
3. Of fragrance have thine oils been excellent;
As oil will be poured forth the name of thee;
Therefore the maidens have been loving thee.
4. Do thou draw me; we after thee will run.
The king hath brought me to his inner halls;
We will rejoice and will be glad in thee;
Will mention thy endearments more than wine:
      Uprightly they have loved thee.
5.   I swarthy am, but comely,
     O daughters of Jerusalem,
      Like as the tents of Kedar,
     Like curtainings of Solomon.
6. O look not ye on me who swarthy am,
On whom hath shone the sun so glaringly!
My mother's children have been wroth at me;
They set me to be keeping the vineyards;
The vineyard of mine own I have not kept.
7. O show to me, thou whom my soul doth love,
     Where is thy herding-ground,
Where wilt thou make the resting-place at noon?
For why should I be as if leprosied,
     Near flocks of thy companions?
8.   *He.* If thou know not, O fair one among women,

Go forth thy way by foot-tracks of the sheep,
And be thou pasturing thy little kids
  Near dwellings of the shepherds.

9. To mine own mare in Pharaoh's chariots
  Have I resembled thee, my friend :

10. O comely are thy cheeks with rows of braid,
  Thy neck with strings of jewels ;

11. Braidings of gold-work we will make for thee,
  Along with studs of silver.

12. *She.* Whene'er the king was present in his court,
  My spikenard gave its fragrance :

13. A bag of myrrh is my beloved to me,
  Between my breasts it lodgeth ;

14. A bunch of henna 's my beloved to me,
  In vineyards of Engedi.

15. *He.* Lo ! thou art fair, my friend ;
  Lo ! thou art fair ; thine eyes are dovelike.

16. *She.* Lo ! my beloved, thou art fair, yea pleasant ;
  Yea, and our couch is flourishing.

17. The beams our houses have are cedar-trees ;
  Our furnishings are cypresses.

CHAPTER II.

1. *He.* I AM a rose of Sharon,
  A lily of the valleys,

2. Like as a lily among jagged thorns,
So will my friend among the daughters be.

3. *She.* Like apricot among the forest trees,
So my beloved is among the sons :
I in his shade desirously have sat ;
Also his fruit was sweet unto my taste.

4. He hath brought me into the house of wine,
Also his banner over me is love.

5. Be ye upholding me with raisin-cakes ;

Be ye refreshing me with apricots ;
Because that sickening of love am I.

6. May his left hand be underneath my head,
And may his right hand be embracing me.

7.   *He.* I have adjured you,
O daughters of Jerusalem,
By the roe-does, or by the hinds of field,
That ye may neither waken nor rouse up
Such love until it be her own delight.

8. *She.* The voice of my beloved ! Lo, he comes !
Leaping along the mountain sides,
Clipping across the little hills :

9. Most like is my beloved to a roe,
Or to a young fawn of the harts :
Behold him as he stands behind our wall,
Intently, from the windows looking in,
Displaying brightly from the lattices !

10. Responding, my beloved said to me,
" Arise thou, O my friend, my fairest one,
And come thy way !

11.   For lo ! the winter is overpast ;
The rain hath shifted, hath gone its course ;

12.   The showy flowers are seen on the earth ;
The time of music hath now come nigh,
And the turtle's voice is heard in our land.

13.   The fig tree ripens its early fruit,
And the vines in bloom give fragrance forth.
Arise thou, O my friend, my fairest one,
And come thy way ! "

14.   *He.* Thou dove of mine, in nest-holes of the crag,
In secret of the precipice,
O let me thine appearance see ;
O let me hear the voice of thee ;
Because thy voice is pleasing,
And thine appearance comely.

15. Do ye catch up for us the foxes,
        The foxes, little ones, which spoil vineyards,
            And our vineyards in bloom.
16.   *She.* O my beloved's mine, and I am his ;
        He shepherdeth among the lilies.
17.   Until the day breeze blow,
                And shadows have fled off,
        Turn, my beloved, be thou like a roe,
            Or like a young fawn of the harts
                Upon the Bether mountains.

CHAPTER III.

1.   *She.* WHEN lying on my bed throughout the nights,
        I oft had sought him whom my soul doth love;
        I sought him eagerly, but found him not.
2. O let me rise, and go about the city ;
        Throughout the lanes, and in the broader streets,
        I shall be seeking him my soul doth love !
        I sought him eagerly, but found him not.
3. The watchmen found me in their city rounds ;
        "Him whom my soul is loving have you seen?"
4. 'Twas but a little I had passed from them,
        Until I found him whom my soul doth love.
        I held by him, and would not let him go,
        'Till I had brought him to my mother's house,
                To my conceiver's chamber.
5.   I have adjurèd you,
            O daughters of Jerusalem,
        By the roe-does, or by the hinds of field,
        That ye may neither waken nor rouse up
        Such love until it be her own delight.

6. What's this upcoming from the wilderness,
            Like stately trees of smoke,

Perfumed with myrrh and frankincense beyond
    All powders of the merchant?

7. Behold! the litter which is Solomon's!
With threescore mighty men surrounding it,
    Of mighty men of Israel?

8.   All of them handlers of the sword,
      Well tutored men of war,
    Each with his sword upon his thigh
      Because of dread by nights.

9. A car king Solomon made for himself
    Of wood from Lebanon:

10. The pillars thereof made he silver,
The cushion gold, the horse-cloth purple;
    The middle of it paved with love
    From daughters of Jerusalem.

11. Go forth, ye Zion daughters, and look well
    At the king Solomon,
With crown whereby his mother did crown him
    In day of his espousals,
    In day of gladness of his heart.

CHAPTER IV.

1.   *He.* Lo! thou art fair, my friend; lo! thou art fair;
Thine eyes be dovelike from within thy veil;
The hair of thee is like a flock of goats
Which have come trooping from Mount Gilead:

2. Thy teeth are like a flock of new-shorn ewes,
Which have come upward from the washing-place,
    Which all of them have gotten twins,
    And no bereft one is among them.

3. Like thread of scarlet are the lips of thee,
    Also thy speech is comely:
Like slice of pomegranate thy temples are,
    Seen from within thy veil;

4. Like tower of David is the neck of thee,
        Built for a place of armour ;
    A thousand shields upon it are hung up,
    All emblems of the mighty men.

5. Thy couple breasts are like a couple fawns,
        The twins of a roe-doe.
    Which pasture find among the lilies.

6.   Until the day-breeze blow,
        And shadows have fled off,
    I will betake me to the mount of myrrh,
    And to the little hill of frankincense.

7.   Entirely fair art thou, my friend ;
        And blemish there is none in thee.

8.   With me from Lebanon, O bride,
    With me from Lebanon, O wilt thou come ?
    Wilt thou be viewing from Amana top,
    From top of Shenir and of Hermon hills,
            From the abodes of lions,
            From mountains of the leopards ?

9. Thou hast inhearted me, my sister, bride ;
    Thou dost enheart me with one of thine eyes,
    With even one chain of thy necklacing.

10. How fair be thine endearments, sister, bride !
    How good be thy endearments more than wine !
    And fragrance of thine oils more than all spice !

11. Sweet droppings from thy lips will come, O bride
    Honey and milk are underneath thy tongue ;
        And fragrance of thy garments is
        Like fragrant smell of Lebanon.

12. A garden lockfast is my sister, bride ;
    A spring-head lockfasted, a fountain sealed.

13. Thy shoots a paradise of pomgranates,
        Along with fruits of preciousness,
        Henna along with spikenard-plants.

14.   Spikenard, and saffron too,
     And cane, and cinnamon,
   Along with all the trees of frankincense ;
     Of myrrh and lign-aloes,
   Along with all the chiefest kinds of spice.

15. A fount of gardens, well of living waters,
 And flowing streams from out of Lebanon.

16. *She.* Awake, thou north wind, and come in, thou south !
 Breathe on my garden till its spices flow !
 Will my beloved to his garden come,
 That he may eat his fruits of preciousness !

CHAPTER V.

1. *He.* I HAVE come to my garden, my sister, bride ;
 I have pluckt my myrrh along with my spice ;
 I have eaten my comb along with my honey ;
 I have drunk my wine along with my milk ;
   Eat ye, O friends ;
 Drink to sufficiency, O ye beloved.

2. *She.* Though I was sleepy, yet my heart did wake.
  A voice ! tis my beloved knocking !
 " O do thou ope to me, my sister, friend,
   My dove, my perfect one !
 Because my head hath become filled with dew,
 My hairlocks with the drizzlings of the night."

3. I having laid my dress aside,
  O wherefore should I put it on ?
  I having cleanly washed my feet,
  O why should I be soiling them ?

4. My loved one sent his hand in from the latch,
 And so my feelings were disturbed for him.

5. I rose, myself to ope for my beloved ;
  And mine own hands were dropping myrrh,
  Also my fingers liquid myrrh
   Upon the handles of the lock.

6. Open did I myself for my beloved ;
   But my beloved had withdrawn, passed on :
   My soul went outward into his request :
   I sought him eagerly, but found him not ;
   I called him, but he did not answer me.

7. The watchmen found me in their city rounds,
         They smote me, wounded me :
   They took away my veil from upon me,
         Those watchmen of the wall.

8.   I have adjured you,
     O daughters of Jerusalem,
   If ye be finding my beloved one,
         That ye shall show to him,
   How sickening of love am I become.

9. *Women.* What's thy beloved more than other loved ?
         O fair one among women ;
   What's thy beloved more than other loved ?
         That thus thou art adjuring us.

10.   *She.* O my beloved clear and ruddy is,
          Distinguished o'er ten thousand :

11.   His head is purest, finest gold ;
      His hairlocks hanging gracefully
          Are swarthy like the raven :

12. His eyes, like doves beside the water dells
          Are bathing amid milk,
          Are set in prominence.

13. His cheeks are like a thriving bed of spice,
          Like towers of mixt perfumes ;
      The lips of him, which lilies be,
          Are dropping liquid myrrh ;

14.   His hands have rings of shining gold,
          Full set with beryl stones ;
      His body of smooth ivory,
          With sapphires over-lined ;

15. His legs as marble pillars be,
    And founded upon sockets of fine gold.
    Appearance of him is like Lebanon,
        As choice as are the cedar-trees.
16. The palate of him is most sweet,
    And he entirely is desirable.
    Such my beloved is, and such my friend,
        O daughters of Jerusalem.

CHAPTER VI.

1. *Women.* WHICH way did thy beloved go,
    O fair one among women?
    Which way did thy beloved turn?
    And we with thee will seek him.
2. *She.* Down to his garden my beloved went,
    Down to the thriving beds of spice,
    To act as shepherd mid the gardens,
        And to be gleaning lilies.
3. O, I for my beloved am,
    And my beloved is for me ;
    He is the shepherd mid the lilies.
4. *He.* O fair art thou, my friend, as Tirzah is ;
    Art comely as Jerusalem ;
    Art terrible as bannered hosts.
5. Be turning round thine eyes from fronting me,
    For they, they overcome me :
    The hair of thee is like a flock of goats,
    Which have come trooping from the Gilead :
6. The teeth of thee are like a flock of ewes
    Which have come upward from the washing-place,
        Which all of them have gotten twins,
        And no bereft one is among them.
7. *He.* Like slice of pomegranate thy temples are,
        Seen from within thy veil.

F

8.   Threescore may they be who are queens,
          And fourscore may be concubines
          And maidens numberless may be ;
9. The one is she, my dove, my perfect one ;
          The one is she to her own mother,
          Pure is she to her who gave her birth.
          The daughters seeing her, will hail her happy ;
          The queens and concubines, they too will praise her.
10. Who may be she, forth-looking like the dawn,
                As fair as is the moon,
                As pure as is the sun,
          As terrible as bannered hosts ?
11. Down to the walnut garden I did go
          To see throughout the springtime of the vale,
          To see what growth was making in the vine,
              How brightly bloomed the pomgranates.
12. I had not known, my soul was setting me
              The chariots of Ammi-nadib.
13. Do thou return, return, O Shulamite !
          Return, return, that we may gaze on thee !
          What will ye gaze at in the Shulamite ?
          As 'twere a dancing of the twofold host.

CHAPTER VII.

1. *He.* How fair have been thy footsteppings in shoes,
                O daughter of Nadib !
          The roundings of thy sides like ornaments,
                Wrought by a skilful hand :
2.   *   *⎫
          *   *⎪
          *   *⎬   (proper translation difficult.)
          *   *⎭

3. Thy couple breasts are like a couple fawns,
              The twins of a roe-doe ;

4. Thy neck is like a tower of ivory ;
   The eyes of thee are pools in Heshbon set,
       Near gateway of Bath-rabbim ;
   Thy nose is like the tower of Lebanon
       Which looks toward Damascus :
5. Thine head upon thee like to Carmel is,
   And fillet of thy head like purple is ;
   The king is bound amid the broideries.
6. How fair, and O how pleasant thou hast been,
   O love, in fulness of delightsomeness !
7. Thy stature now is like to a palm tree,
       And thy breasts like to clusters.
8. I said, I will climb into the palm tree,
   I will take hold upon the fronds of it ;
       And O that thine own breasts may be
       Like clusters of the vine !
   And fragrance of thy nose like apricots !
9. And may thy palate be like that good wine
   Which goes to my beloved suitably,
   Which moistens lips of them who are asleep !
10. *She.* I my beloved's am,
       And upon me is his desire.
11. Come, my beloved ! let us go afield ;
       Let us be lodging in the hamlets ;
12.   Let us be early at the vineyards ;
       Let us see how the vine is growing
           To ope its fragrant bud ;
       How brightly bloom the pomgranates.
   There my endearments I will give to thee.
13. The mandrakes have given a fragrance forth ;
   And close by our doors be all precious things ;
       New things together with old,
   Beloved of mine, I have stored for thee.

CHAPTER VIII.

1. *She.* O THAT thou wert as brother unto me,
   One who did suck my mother's breasts !
   I would find thee outside, I would kiss thee ;
   Yea, none should be despising me.
2.   I would lead thee ;
   I would bring thee toward my mother's house ;
         She would teach me :
   I would cause thee to drink of wine well-spiced,
   Of fresh juice of my pomgranate.
3. May his left hand be underneath my head,
   And may his right hand be embracing me !
4.   I have adjured you,
         O daughters of Jerusalem,
   Why should you wake, and why should you rouse up
   Such love until it be her own delight ?
5. Who's this upcoming from the wilderness,
   Leaning herself on her beloved one ?
   Beneath the apricots I roused thee up ;
   There was thy mother strictly pledging thee ;
   There a strict pledge made she who gave thee birth.
6. Do thou set me like seal upon thy heart,
         Like seal upon thine arm ;
   For powerful as death itself is love,
   As keen as Sheol will be jealousy ;
   The shooting darts of it are darts of fire,
         A flashing flame of Jah.
7.   Abounding waters
   Shall not be able to quench out such love ;
   Nor shall the forceful rivers sweep it down :
         If any man would give
   The total substance of his house for love,
         They would outright despise it.

8.   We have a sister, small as yet,
And breasts not fully grown for her;
What shall we do for this our sister
In day she may be spoken of?

9.   If that she be a wall,
Let us build up on her a court of silver;
And if she be a door
Let us fix up on her a board of cedar.

10.   I am a wall,
And mine own breasts like towers be
So I have been in eyes of him
Like one who findeth peace.

11. A vineyard did to Solomon belong
At Baal-Hamon;
He gave the vineyard into keepers' charge,
Each was to bring for fruit thereof
A thousand silver coins.

12. My vineyard which is mine before me is;
The thousand are for thee, O Solomon;
Also two hundred are
For keepers of the fruit thereof.

13. O thou fair sitter mid the gardens,
Companions hearken for the voice of thee;
Do thou cause me to hear.

14.   Speed thou, O my beloved one!
And do resemble thee unto a roe,
Or to a young fawn of the harts
Upon the mounts of spices!

www.ingramcontent.com/pod-product-compliance
Lightning Source LLC
Chambersburg PA
CBHW020039030726

47499CB00007B/2500